WITH YOUR EYES WIDE OPEN

With Your Eyes Wide Open

Stories by
Robert MacIsaac

EVERY BOOK PRESS
MMXII

ISBN 978-0-9837714-1-8

Pen and Ink Drawings: Solee Hampton MacIsaac
Cover Photo: Radu Sava
Book Design: William Bentley

Stories

I opened my eyes very wide. There I had been for all eternity, as it were, and now at last I was coming to life.

Katherine Mansfield

In Flight

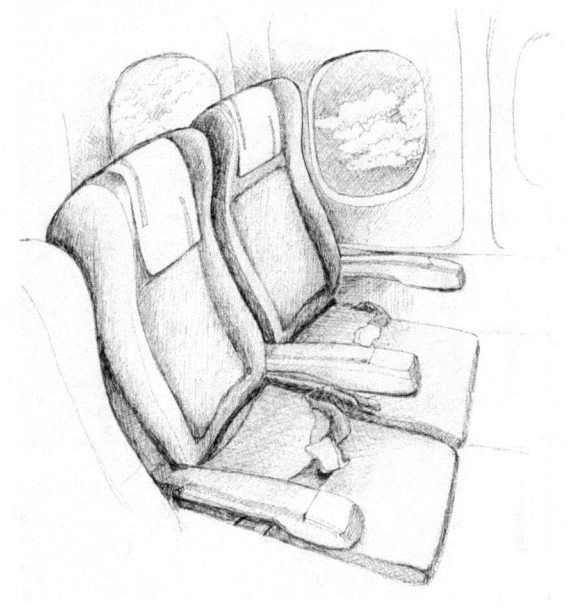

for Jeanne

In Flight

AS ALERT TO THE CHANGES in his temperament as he usually was, Laszlo at that critical juncture was not quite quick enough to check the rising irritation that resulted from his fingers fumbling over, dropping, tugging, pulling at, prying, and eventually conveying to his angrily clenched teeth the slippery plastic sack of ketchup that had resisted his every civilized effort to open it without the use of his now reluctantly prepared jawbone. About seven minutes later it became vividly clear to him that his irritation had imperceptibly commenced when he had entered the front entryway of the airliner, smiled hello to Lise, the senior flight attendant, and then realized, probably because of smiling at Lise, since she knew who he was, that he had left his carry-on luggage on the adjacent seat back in the waiting lounge. It was not that Laszlo begrudged having to cart about such unnecessary baggage; he actually enjoyed the black, all-leather case with gold fittings and embossed lettering, and despite his many years in security and special services, continued to retain a boyish feeling of clandestine excitement in knowing that no one knew who he really was or why he was really on that plane. Of course, these same seven minutes later that contained the understanding as to where and how his irritation

3

started also contained an understanding that rather altered his own conception of who he really was and why he was really on that plane. But prior to the arrival of those said seven minutes, Flight 818 from Reykjavik to Frankfurt contained—to state it once again, at a certain critical juncture—one incensed sky marshal with an embarrassing blob of ketchup dribbling from his lip down over his chin.

The irritation that now flamed alive inside the tanned and muscular frame of this fifty-two year old gentleman did not have its explosiveness conveyed to any of his fellow passengers by means of colorful oaths, banging fists, or even a sharp and heated intake of breath. Mr. Karas's right hand trembled for a moment as it sought a paper napkin to wipe away the annoying sensation of wetness from his face, and when that was accomplished he let out a series of long, low sighs to calm himself while looking past the young man seated next to him and out upon the tundra of silent white cloud. "There are silences," Laszlo reflected as he attempted to bring back silence to his own internal world, "that subsume all the rages of human nature. The stars with their enigmatic patterns, the chasms in the earth's crust, and this perspective of gray and white pasture—one of the privileged vantage points of twentieth-century toil—are not a silence of no sound, but of all sounds. Any distance set a lifetime away from our fingertips can hear, and no doubt had heard, all the weeping and longing and laughter of more than one human heart. The curved borders of our vision and of the cycle of our blood know themselves as mortality only when set against the horizontal and vertical unlimits that life occasionally—and perhaps more than occasionally, if we could but see it—casts in our path."

The relaxation that resulted from these and similar thoughts helped Laszlo to dispel a rather poisonous fog of unpleasant feelings that had clouded his first hour on board the aircraft. He could now outline with a clear mind the schedule of tasks he needed to fulfill after arriving at his final destination in Johannesburg, and he began to reach into his jacket pocket to take out his leather appointment book, when, probably as a result of the slight inclination of his head toward the inside right-hand portion of his suit, he glimpsed out of the corner of his left eye a rather unusual circumstance that, when he turned his full attention upon it, shot him into the state of adrenalized attentiveness that every fiber of his flesh was used to experiencing when an oft anticipated moment of danger becomes the reality of one's own living and breathing present.

Later that day, when the plane landed in Frankfurt, only twelve minutes behind its scheduled arrival time, it was understandable enough that most of the people on board, and many of the journalists who heard and reported about the incident, would place all the blame for what happened on the inattentiveness of sky marshal Laszlo Karas to respond with the sober urgency that such an unusual moment had certainly warranted. But again, to return to our critical juncture on board Flight 818, Mr. Karas, because of his attending momentarily to the personal matter of attempting to control his anger and rid his heart of a few unnecessary acid-like feelings, failed to notice a certain blonde-haired gentleman in a steel gray suit, who had been seated on the aisle just on the other side of the middle exit door of the aircraft from where the sky marshal was seated, stand up, unwind a coil of rope that had been tied to his waist and wrapped round his torso, lash the other end of the rope firmly to the armrest and back of his seat, press the call button to signal for a flight attendant, welcome the arrival of Lise herself with a smile and a severe snatching of her neck under the crook of his arm, remove a black revolver from his jacket pocket and place it to her head, and call out to everyone in the body of the plane over the fitful screams of the terrified young woman that the airplane was now his and that everyone was to stay where they were, or the poor lady he was holding would not be able to scream any longer.

It was the moment containing the snatching of Lise and the removal of the revolver from the pocket that Laszlo had noticed out of the corner of his eye, and it was his full, angered attentiveness that received the audacious declaration of this calm young man to the assembly of frightened passengers and crew members.

A troubled murmur spread through the electrified crowd. Two or three other women screamed; a child in the rear of the plane began crying. The door to the pilot's cabin opened momentarily and closed with a bang. "Everybody shut up!" the hijacker shouted in a high-pitched squeal obviously unnatural to him and gave another yank on Lise's neck. "No one of you fools need make a sound. You are not animals, are you? You are not a gaggle of geese, are you? Or little tiny chicks, or eeny meeny mices?"

The man seemed to grow amused and absorbed by his similes, and Laszlo watched him pause and reopen his grinning mouth, as though to come out with a few more clever phrases, when the voice of the pilot over the loudspeaker system interrupted him: "Please state your objective. Captain Ferguson awaiting your request. All passengers please stay calm." The assailant immediately grew serious and motioned for another flight attendant to draw near. He half-whispered at a pitch Laszlo could not quite catch what seemed to be a new bearing and altitude, and as the attendant hurried toward the front of the plane, the man called after him, "And you may as well stay in there because we're making this trip with the emergency door open." He then rearranged his arms around Lise's waist and nudged her toward the levers that controlled the opening and closing of the middle exit door. "All you people buckle up now, just like it says on the plastic card on the seat pocket in front of you." He chuckled to himself. This character was thoroughly enjoying his monologue. A psychiatrist seated three rows behind sky marshal Karas concluded that the man was subconsciously fulfilling a need to perform before an audience that could give him the assurance of unwavering attention. "At what price satisfaction," this doctor of the mind concluded to himself.

In this same moment Laszlo concluded something different. With a bittersweet sense of relief, he realized that his first intuitive perception was correct. He very slowly and easily let his left arm relax and slip into his lap, and then moved it toward the clasp of the seat belt. Lise meanwhile had removed the plastic casing from around the emergency door's lever, also as slowly as possible. "Come on now, darling, let's get on with it," her captor said and nudged her with his hip. "I've got good hold of you. And, to all of you people up here who need to go to the toilet, I extend to you my deepest sympathy. But business is business. Okay, sweetheart, throw it op..."

Between the sweet and the heart Laszlo was but a few inches from placing his hands round the man's throat. The weapon he had been holding against Lise's head did not look like any revolver that the security officer knew of, and as the man's real threat was holding Lise before an open door, it was obvious that the gun was a dummy. But unmindful of this, most people seated in the vicinity of the two men and captive girl cringed and ducked down as low as possible. Screams and shouts came from all parts of the aircraft. Laszlo's burly fingers pressed and tightened around the young man's throat. The hijacker threw the gun away and lashed out at his opponent with fists and heels. In another moment the sky marshal forced him down and pinned his shoulders to the floor.

Their eyes met. Such anger, such wild confusion, and then, and then such terror! All this did the hijacker see in the pale blue eyes of the broad tanned face bearing down on him. For, as Laszlo had begun to throw his weight forward into his captive, he felt a sudden shudder of wind pierce his eardrums and enmesh his body in a snare of icy gusts that yanked at his ankles, hauled him back and down smack on his face, and drag him along the floor with his nose and lips unjustly pressed into the carpet. In another instant he was flipped upside down, then his hip, then shoulder, then skull banged against the steel frame of the hatchway, and he shot out the door and into the frozen sky, with one final desperate attempt to grab hold of anything solid resulting in the tearing away of two of his fingernails.

Like the abrupt cutting off of a musical recording, Laszlo heard and lost a few horrible shrieks that had reacted to his helpless body hurtling out the doorway. The icy air bit at his face and tore away his clothing. His mouth gaped open and tried to suck some of the precious rushing air into his lungs. His first intake of breath was full of jet fumes. His stomach heaved, his throat and eyes burned, his arms and legs were loose and flailing. He was falling, falling, and again falling. The reflexes in his body kept seeking for pressure and solidity underneath him. But no, he only fell. He saw the dark hulk of the airplane, above him now, gliding away at a slight angle into the damp haze. A stream of smoke lingered in the air. Then two solid puffs appeared in quick succession just above him and quickly spread apart and tumbled oddly downward. The next moment he saw that it was not more smoke, but two other bodies. When he recognized Lise, she was fearfully bound up in her clothing. Her skirt was tangled around her ankles, her blouse had jerked her arms up over her head. A moment later the clothing was ripped away. The other figure fell almost motionless by comparison. A long cord snarled aloft from the body's midsection, making it look like a new-born babe plunging from some stellar womb down into the lower depths of gravity and flesh. So justice kept its place. The hijacker, whom records showed to have registered for Flight 818 under the name of Sealton, now locked himself into a numb refusal to experience his new, his final, predicament. With limbs as rigid as the velocity of air under him allowed, he tried to fix his eyes far away into the deep blue above him. The wiggling line of rope still bound around his waist served him for a guide or crosshair by which he attempted to peer deeper and further into the sky overhead. He knew there were stars out there. He knew there were friendly twinkles. Only the curve of light from the bright morning sun prevented him from seeing them. But surely they saw him. They saw him lying there. Lying on his air mattress, his bed of cloudy down, just lying there, just lying. Surely one of those friendly twinkles would soon wink at him. Surely they would. And when he winked back, then a star-clustered arm would reach through the mist and snatch up the cord. That is what would happen. That is why he put the cord out there anyway. That was the real reason. No better way to attract a divinity. No better way at all. It could easily happen, and it would be invisible to mortal eyes. We could not see it. But it would happen anyway. I think it is happening now. I think so. I no longer seem to be moving. And the blue is getting darker. Darker and darker. Soon it will get black. Then I will see their twinkling eyes. Pulling me up. Pulling me onto the zodiac shore. I am a fish. A fish for the gods. Fishy, fishy, fishy.

Laszlo momentarily resented the sight of that motionless body. "Why should he sleep? Why should he be allowed repose at such a terrible moment, while Lise and I hurtle wide-eyed through the cruel atmosphere?" The two questions came and fled. Laszlo was relieved that they did so. They disappeared not so much by his own efforts to dispel them, but more because the blizzard that was now his mind and heart sent fragments of fear, awe, love, speculation and dreams whirling in and away from his awareness like the dry captives of a hurricane wind. He tried for a moment to twist his body around with arms pointed straight down, head bowed, and legs thrust taut into the sky, as though a diver's position would somehow give him an advantage when he reached the sea. The silliness of the idea wriggled through his frame rather rapidly. He could not close his arms, he could not really move them at all. He managed to swing his head down. He stared at the translucent white vapors below that oozed eastward in the stiff breeze. And through the mist he saw more and thicker billows expanding and congealing, the clumps of fluff nuzzling and nosing like frightened lambs back into their own mass. And below these he could see a wide dun-colored film. Flat and firm. The belt around his waist shook and snapped. His trousers shot down to his thighs. They became entangled there since his legs could not close. The freezing wet air cut into his loins. Chills ran from his spine to his skull. All through this journey the air lashed at each of these poor folk. Their skin became redder and rawer. Lise, almost naked, would have shuddered for freezing were it not for the vigorous beating of the wind against her muscles, clamped and rigid. For some moments she too searched for solidity. She wished, in her helplessness, for a warm pair of arms to hold her. Warm strong arms around her shoulders, her face pressed against his chest. Warm and firm. Long and quiet breaths. The rise and fall of their chests lulling each other to sleep. Why was she not married? Why had she not stayed in London? She did not love Anson. No, but to be there now, to be holding him, so safe and solid.

In the next instant her hair blew away out of her eyes, and her glance happened to meet the eyes of Laszlo. They were about six feet apart, she falling horizontally on her belly, and he below her falling vertically upside down. His loose clothing fluttered madly about his frame and concealed the view of most of his face, but through the flailing pieces of cloth she saw his eyes. Here was something that did not move. Human contact, a link established through the gentlest organ and most tender energies that man and woman know. Here was the meaning of the eternal stars, the lidless watchful repose of evening, that knew the rise and fall of human passion, that saw the thousands of sexual meetings rocking in unison in the dark, this rocking the galaxy of human love that shone back up at the immortals. Here was a meeting of two souls, each at the window of its own frightened vessel.

Lise felt all of these things at once, and felt as well that Laszlo knew and understood them in the same way. And she was not far wrong. For as he had plummeted downward and continued to examine the film of the earth that gradually began to heave up colored patches and ridges and runnels in its surface, his head suddenly jerked upward and, through the rollick of his shredding trousers, engaged the soft brown eyes of his long-time friend. Her hair was standing straight up, and her flesh was deep pink and almost glowing. Despite himself, Laszlo could not resist a momentary fancy of the two of them reaching out, grasping each other's hands, pulling themselves together, and, against the rude wishes of gravity, enjoying a final interlocking. He could not tell if any glimmer of this was communicated to her, but soon the terror in her eyes revived his own, and from then on the recognition of his true helplessness never left him.

It was in this same moment that an interesting rapport became established. For Lise and Laszlo began to converse. This was obviously not in any conventional sense, because it never occurred to either one of them to attempt to move their lips or diaphragms or facial muscles. But like the semaphores of light that ships at evening or castaways on a distant island flash at one another across unfathomable horizons, the glints of emotion and impressions that burbled through these sorry companions were caught up and recognized by the other, and then each in turn, by directing their own thoughts toward the impression they had just received from the other's eyes, were able to carry on what was conceivably one of the most rapid exchanges in the realm of human experience. Each wink was a world, every new shade of emotion a twenty-minute discourse. Laszlo began by thanking Lise for reminding him of his mortality and went on to praise any accident that threatened our lives as the only great opportunity to return to a sense of our true helplessness in the face of infinity. Lise demurred at this proclamation, since it was touching to recognize the humility with which Mr. Karas succumbed to the moment. But she then went on to point out that the joys of love contained a similar lesson. Our vulnerability and need for affection, our efforts to care for another's wishes and not our own, the sweetness between two hearts that made so many common moments glisten—was this not just as deep, nay, a deeper lesson of our smallness and of the vast sea of love within which our awkward efforts to paddle about could only make us grateful for any chance to participate in the great lessons of eternity? Laszlo was overwhelmed and wanted at once to give a gesture of his gratitude. He started to raise one arm toward her, but as Galileo had so long ago demonstrated, she could not move closer to him nor he to her. She suggested that he let go of the idea anyway, for his gesture had been warmly received. Laszlo enjoyed this yielding feeling, and went on into a confession of some of the grievous errors of his past. He shuffled before Lise's patient gaze a stream of self-abuse, monologues that had belonged to his solitary rages, undetected compromises with his real desires and aims, in short, every regret that he had ever experienced. He perhaps would have persisted in his apparently honest confessions, when Lise interrupted him with a sudden surprised gesture at something that appeared to be just below him. He gasped and winced, and with a great flexing of his neck and shoulder he pushed his head straight down, the blood now throbbing around his eyes and temples. At this altitude crosswinds began to emerge, and Laszlo rocked and shuddered to and fro, forced into a madcap dance that confounded his efforts to see what Lise saw. He squinted, gasped, tried to hold himself as tightly as possible, stared again, searched the whistling chaos, searched his own mind for clues to what she saw.

Two winds now tore crazily about him, the wilder one inside his head. How mad the words, the pictures, the memories. Memories, always, even now, with that same sweet allure, how he longed for something soft, or joyous, or himself a hero, and how the sweet allure so swiftly shows itself as not a memory at all; no, that did not happen, that did not happen—what did not happen? It is gone. I want another. My days in the wood. Fresh dank grass, hissing leaves, moonglow on them. I am falling! Shudders fill his spine, his limbs. Another memory. When was that? Was I young? I am young. I am the same. Another thought. Thought is not memory. I want to talk about my life. Again he could not breathe. The gasps for air so futile, so brutal, so ignorant of who he was. He was—he was that month in the forest, the far-off little village of polished grey stone. He never liked books. Only the smell. The smell was good. They say your life should pass before you now, but all I see is what I always see. This always passes before me, and after it passes what is left? I am still here. So am I my life? If so, where did I pass to? It always did this, nothing new, the only difference is I could take a book and smell it, or take a train to the forest. I thought of it in the taxi here. Not here. The terminal. To the terminal. Leather seats smell good too.

But abruptly this all stopped. What did she mean? He let his chin drop to his breast. How it hurt his neck. But he wanted to find her, ask her. He scanned the air above, his trousers now shredded to wisps, no longer obstructing his gaze. But how he wished he had not looked up! Above him nothing but grey cold mist, pushing down on him, pushing, pressing, impenetrable billows of cold smoke, all but insisting he forget about looking skyward: "See you cannot! Nothing up here! Down, down you go!" Desperately he looked about. He started to shout with his eyes. She would hear. She had to hear.

And his vision shouted and shouted, and amid that hail of wind—and now rain, cold, wet, fiery wet rain—a still open space in the rushing tumult, a hole, no larger than a fingerprint, un-moving, silent, awe-full, fathomless, drew in his gaze and, for the briefest whisper of time, both answered every terror and dissolved every assurance. This hole, no, two holes, motionless, there, not falling, just above the level of his gaze, into them he delved and delved, and yearned to crawl into their silent, safe emptiness; and only after moments he could not number did these twin orbs seem to gush a plume of flesh and flailing riot about them, and only then did he see that these fathomless holes were Lise's eyes. Where was she? How had she shifted, tumbled perhaps, in her inner world into an unknown angle of space, a movement some-where far from this falling, terrible falling, nothing under him, nothing. He snatches up at his knees, he kicks out, only empty, only vicious slices of frigid air-blades everywhere, only down and down and down. Where is she? Where?

Where she is he suddenly knew. Everything battered sav-agely his body, this lawless world where bodies should not be. But here, where he so thoroughly did not belong, despite this unending punishment, undeniable outcome, unmoving plummet to oblivion, just now he understood what she had been indicating to him. It was nothing below; it was nothing else at all. He wanted to explain it to himself, and to her, but Lise's immutable fixity quelled every cogitation the moment it arose. And so he gazed with her, at this, at where they now stood. Yes, stood, stood here, in this moment in time, in this personal moment of their lives. How it washed over him, the feeling, or rather a presence, deeper than a feeling, that all of our life is like this; always are we standing on a bottomless abyss, the abyss of forward time, not to be stopped, not to be controlled. Always are we screaming forward, no footfall rests on something solid, always it dissolves, every innocent daydream, or idle chat wine glass in hand, or all-night meetings and hurried meals, or rush down the stairs, or saunter down the stairs, fast or slow matters not, it is always too fast, it all passes and passes and we sleep, and we wake and off the covers come and how can we stop it, the screaming forward, we can't, we can't stop it, and we can't because we don't want to, because we think the answer will be in the next screaming, flying second or day or year, the answer will be there, the goal, and so we fly on, not stopping, not stopping. Yet stop it they did, Lise and Laszlo, the simplest and only way, here they stood, just now, and saw each other and themselves, and here, yes, was the sidelong angle that Lise had found into another world, and he followed her there, and they stood and witnessed the screaming forward hurtle of time; and this standing and looking and being, and the foment of love they shared, led to an understanding that reminded Laszlo of the momentary calm reflection he experienced just as he managed to release his anger (how grateful he felt for that!) those few precious moments before the aircraft drama unfolded—a drama that led to a six-month investigation into how Sealton (not his real name) got on the plane with a plastic gun (he assembled it while in his seat), why he did it (money), whether he was connected to a terrorist organization (he was not), and what on earth he was thinking to assume a passenger jet could travel with an emergency hatch open (no doubt a boyhood fantasy); and led to many, many articles, interviews and documentaries on the "818 Miracles," the first miracle that remained so because it was never satisfactorily comprehended how the emergency door that the flight attendant unlatched somehow slid part way open, discharged three startled victims, then snapped back shut such that it threw bodies forward but caused no further injuries other than a psychiatrist cracking one of his front teeth on an armrest, the second miracle the prowess of Captain Ferguson to negotiate the precarious angle the plane was forced into for several miles until he was able to set it right and realign his bearings, all the while a silent tense fear among the passengers as the tilting aircraft shuddered through the skies for what seemed hundreds and hundreds of precious unbearable minutes; and led to a book that recreated all of the drama of that fateful morning, the book the result of interviews with every single passenger and crew member, the many points of view cleverly woven together in fine imaginative prose; and led to memorial services for the two victims, the one remembered for her welcoming charm and many years of service in the skies, the other praised for his heroism but questioned for the many secret missions he had undertaken which no one knew of and no agency cared to mention—to this infinite present moment, aware of but outside of time and its trappings, aware such that a feeling arose, like a flowering bulb of pure flame, that pervaded their flesh and hearts and minds, a bliss not unlike the proverbial feeling of walking ten feet off the ground.

The Tumbler Problematical

for Professor Whiteside

The Tumbler Problematical

"**T**RYING TO SIP THAT WATER in a casual manner is not going to explain away the whole problem just like that, Doctor Murphy! I assure you, the time for glib responses is over!"

I shouted these last words with such triumphant finality that the good man nearly choked on the liquid he was, at this very moment, pouring from that renegade object into his seldom unloquacious mouth. But he just as quickly recovered his composure and continued sipping away, attempting, against all reason and common decency, to remain perfectly calm and completely oblivious to my last determined remark.

"You cannot, I repeat, *can not* tell me, that this little cylinder of glass which, aside from the occasional tipping of your wrist, remains as motionless and inanimate as all the slugs in Central Asia, you cannot tell me that this thing is moving! Moving? Where is it moving? Where? Just look at it! Look! Look!"

It was a bit difficult for him to comply with this rather heated request of mine just at that moment, as he was tilting his head back against the chair and gargling a large mouthful of water, all the time staring intently at the brass chandelier on the ceiling, but also, and this did not escape my attention, looking at me with some curious disdain now and then out of the corner of one eye.

"Doctor, will you please be so kind as to desist from this fountainous rebuke and answer my question." I realized then that the calm approach had distinct advantages in a situation like this. And it worked, because no sooner had I said these words than he swallowed the water, let out a contented sigh, and a little burp, straightened himself up, extended his right arm and triumphantly tilted the glass so that its full eight inches of length were perfectly parallel to the plane of the carpeted floor underneath our feet. That is to say, he started pouring water all over the place.

"What are you doing! Stop! Stop it!"

I snatched the tumbler out of his hands and placed it firmly on the table. The Doctor stared at me through his thick, blackrimmed glasses with the learned perusal of intellectual contempt. And I, for my part, returned a likewise optical expression.

"My dear Doctor Murphy, are you not aware that at this precise moment that water is seeping through this quarter inch of carpeting, oozing its way in between the cracks of the floorboards underneath, and creating a gentle pool of liquid that will, at some future unknown appointed moment, slip out through a chink in the ceiling below and commence drip-dripping in a steady stream onto the floor beneath this one?"

"Yes."

"Then why, may I ask, and I ask purely for the purposes of improving my knowledge of the situation and of yourself, why in God's name did you do it?"

"I didn't want anymore."

I was aghast.

"You are aghast."

"Wha—what?"

"You *are*... are aghast. You should be using the present tense. It's happening now, isn't it?"

"Well... uh... yes. Yes, of course! But if I explain it to someone else, I use the past tense. That's obvious!"

"Why?"

"Because it happened. It was. So it's the past. It's all perfectly clear. Something happens now, and then, it's over. It's the past. I tell someone else, I say 'It was' or 'It did' or 'It had been,' or even..."

"But this is sheer nonsense, my friend." As he said this, he stretched out his arms and legs luxuriously in his brown leather chair, just like a contented cat about ready to doze off. Then he opened his mouth and emitted the most drawn out, relaxed yawn any civilized human being is likely to witness. I felt like punching him in the stomach.

"Yes, yes," he murmured. "Absolute, unadulterated gaar-baage..."

"But how else can you describe the past? It's all slipping away from us as quickly as we open our mouths to capture it... even quicker, really. Just think of it, Doctor! As soon as something happens, it's gone. You can't call it back. You can't even talk about it in all its details. Something's always left out. So we're left with 'I did this' and 'I saw that' because, quite obviously, what we're talking about is not what we're doing—Well, no, we are talking about it, that *is* what we're doing then, but the thing we're describing is not what we're doing, but what we did."

"So the past only exists in our memory of it."

"Precisely."

"And what about the present?"

"The present? This is the present. It exists now."

"And when does it become the past?"

"When it's over."

He raised his eyebrows and stared at me again, this time *over* his glasses. "When the present is over? Is that what you mean?" I noted a few distinct traces of mirth beginning to appear in twitches at the corners of his mouth.

"No! Of course not! When the thing that's happening *in* the present is over. Then it's the past."

"How do you know when it's over?"

"How? When it's finished! When it's no longer here! Now come on, Doctor, this is all rather fundamental, isn't it?"

"Yes, yes, indeed," he chuckled softly to himself as he pulled up his socks and retied his shoes.

He finished cleaning the other lens, stuffed his handkerchief back into his pocket, and put his glasses back on.

"Where were you just then?"

"…who… me? Here, where else?"

Again he started chuckling, this time covering his mouth with his hands, as though to conceal this from me. But soon he was shaking with uncontrollable laughter for several minutes as the tears poured down his cheeks.

"Where is here?" he finally blurted out from between wet fingers.

Against all rational behavior, against all moralistic sense of decorum, decency and proper Christian ethics, against every desire to please, placate, assist and indulge my fellow human be-ing, I wanted above all else in that moment to grab the so-called good Doctor by the lapels of his brown tweed jacket and give him the soundest thrashing this side of the Indian Ocean!

"Here is here!" I screamed. "Here! Here! Here! Here!"

"Yes—I hear!" he cackled, nearly suffocating under the blanket of laughs and guffaws he is now indulging in.

Suddenly he stopped.

"That's right! That's it! I am *now* indulging in them. Now. Not indulged. Indulging. Now."

"Yes, that's what I just said."

He looked at me very intently. Then he leaned back in his chair again and, without taking his eyes off me, said, "You still haven't told me where you were while I was tying my shoes and cleaning my glasses."

We must be patient, I said to myself, we must try to un-derstand. "Well, Doctor," I said with a slightly quavering voice, "I was sitting here the whole time. Here, on this ottoman. So

I must have been here. All the same, I suppose I didn't quite notice every particular thing you were doing. I mean, after all, why should I?" This last remark seemed to make the most sense to me, so I emphasized it as adroitly as possible in order for him to see my point.

"No, no, indeed. But of course, 'should' has nothing to do with it, really. Anymore than it does for this tumbler here."

He pointed to that glass culprit, standing between us on the walnut end table as indifferent as the moon.

"Well, wait now. I never said the tumbler should do any-thing—except perhaps to stay perpendicular to the floor." I couldn't help throwing in that little jibe at the end.

Doctor Murphy gazed at it with serene dignity. "Yes, yes. It is more attractive this way, I must admit. But," he sighed, "let me try to explain my position once again. And please, Jeremy, please make the effort to take it all in as calmly as you can. Okay?"

"Okay. But all the same, I don't know why you call me Jeremy, when my name is Roger."

"Do you like the name Jeremy?"

"Does it matter."

"Now, Jeremy, can you recall what I was saying before you lost your temper?"

This stung me right in the chest. "Must you refer to the past in that way?"

"Ah, ah, ah. There you go again. But you see, that's not quite accurate. I wasn't referring to the past. This is my whole point."

I sighed and leaned back in my own chair, and then watched the wall fly up to the ceiling as I landed on my ba... "Ow!"

The doctor howled like a hyena being tickled by an orang-utan and a baboon at the same time.

"You can't lean back very far on an ottoman, eh, Jeremy! Probably no more than twelve degrees, I should think."

"Never mind! Never mind!" I shouted. But I didn't really mean it. Somehow I felt too humiliated to be angry. Instead I just flung myself full length on the couch, propped myself up on one elbow, and looked steadily at my impossible companion.

"Comfy?"

"Enough."

"Now, let's review what I said before. Movement in space is simply an adjunct of movement in time. In actual fact, movement in space *is* movement in time. Real movement is in time. But, time doesn't move—not without our participation at any rate. If we consider an object, any object, but, for the purposes of this discussion, and the title of this story of yours, this tumbler here, we can deduce that, as it sits here, seemingly oblivious to all that goes on around it, just as you were a few moments ago, my boy, indeed, not even in any way cognizant of what is going on around it, at least, not in the way we human beings, or, for that matter, other warm-blooded mammals, and, in actual fact, cold-blooded reptiles as well, are, it still is, because of the special relationship of it, the object, to us, the perceivers of the object, both of whom maintain an equally special relationship to space, and, of course, to time, which, as we have already noted, is, in actuality, the precursor of space, moving."

Just in that moment I couldn't quite remember the capital of North Dakota.

"Now, we may ask, and indeed we, in point of fact, *should* ask (as distinct from my previous remark ((about two pages back)) that we should not 'should' this tumbler, or our own personal attitude, toward why we are or are not aware of 'every particular thing' ((to use your own expression, Jeremy)), which, in actuality, is a different type of 'should,' which we all should be aware of by now) why it is that we will react so violently to the suggestion that this poor little innocent tumbler is moving, when, as far as we, with our usual blasé appraisal of the external world, can surmise, this humble translucent creation is not inching one infinitesimal, miniscule iota from its present location. And, as an obvious corollary to the foregoing, we may also enquire as to why we will emit a sigh of metaphysical relief when the good Doctor Murphy takes the tumbler thus"—

He took it—

"Holds it up to the light for all of us to see clearly"—

He held it up—

"Turns to face the open drawing room window"—

He turned and faced it—

"And heaves it with all the strength he can muster!"

He threw it—right out the window!

"Oh!" I shot up on the couch like a freedom seeking spring and bounced at him in anger. "Oh! Doctor, No!"

"My word, Jeremy. I wouldn't exactly call that a sigh of metaphysical relief!"

"You might have hit someone in the head..."

"Were you able to follow that well enough?"

"...or frightened some children..."

"Any more questions before I proceed?"

"...they're going to think we're drunk..."

"Good. It becomes obvious then that what is needed above all else is a reassessment of the way in which we perceive movement. This is especially critical in lieu of the fact that you are probably going to exhaust yourself coming up with possible consequences as to our immediate future after seeing our precious tumbler travel about fourteen yards out of our sight in a southeasterly direction with an approximate velocity of twenty-one miles per hour." He raised his hand before I could offer an objection—to which I object, because I wasn't going to offer one, even though I should have—and proceeded. "Let us suppose, then, that the tumbler had not been removed from its previous position, but instead had remained standing here for one full hour, untouched and undisturbed. Now—what would happen then?"

"Nothing."

"Wrong. The tumbler would proceed on its merry way through time. The tumbler would move, as in fact we are, and everything else around us is."

"But no! When you threw the tumbler, that was *real* movement! It flew through the air and out the window..."

"...at that moment in time. And at this moment in time, I am scratching my head." He scratched his head.

I really couldn't believe this. "This is fantasy! This all depends on our own subjective perceptions! I look at my watch, I see that an hour has gone by, and I say to myself, 'My word, an hour's gone by,' and..."

"Really, Jeremy, you must try to get rid of that awful habit of talking to yourself."

"Well, no one else will listen to me! Especially you!!" I am sorry, ladies and gentlemen, but sometimes my own intellectual zeal catapults me against my better judgment into awkward moments of severe impoliteness. This was one of them.

"This *is* one of them."

"Oh, all right then! This *is* one of them!"

"So, Jeremy," he continued, "you think that just because that little metal dial on your wrist is spinning around, you can thereby assume that the tumbler was not, in some way, moving as well?"

"Well, if it was, I certainly didn't see it."

"But when I tossed it out the window, you did see it move?"

"Of course! Didn't you?"

"And how far had your little dial moved from the moment the tumbler left my hand to the moment it disappeared from our sight?"

This was really unfair. "I didn't notice that! It happened too fast. I barely had time to sit up on the couch, much less register how many seconds went by."

Doctor Murphy slowly shook his head. "So really what you're saying is that it happened too fast for you to think of looking, and then actually look, at your watch to observe how many of your so-called seconds went by?"

"Yes. But that's not so important in this context, is it? I mean, what I was really reacting to were the consequences of what would happen when that tumbling tumbler tumbled onto whatever it tumbled onto."

"And what are those consequences?"

"Well, we don't know that yet!"

You may have seen on a hot summer's day an exhausted postman unloading a truck full of large canvas bags filled with letters, cards, magazines, catalogs, and other printed matter. And, as the sweat poured from his brow and chest, and his breathing became more labored, you may have witnessed him take the final sack and, trembling under its weight and his own exhaustion, let it fall with a loud and clumsy thud onto the pavement. Well, it was like unto such a sack of post that the good Doctor just now crashed to the floor and began once again roaring with the laughter of a thousand circus clowns and their boisterous audience.

"Ah ha ha ha ha ha ha ha ha ha ha ha ha! Ah ha ha ha ha ha ha ha ha ha ha ha!"

There is little doubt that I was nearly on the verge of firing a volley of tumblers, cushions, picture frames, lamps, chairs and whatever else I could get hold of right at the cause of this outrage to my honor, my respect, my intellectual reputation, and my newly carpeted floor, were it not for the timely entrance of that eternal figurehead and symbol of the innocent stander by and otherwise unobtrusive observer of life's daily to-ings and fro-ings—the postman himself.

"I have something rather curious here, Roger, something curious indeed. In fact, I believe it must have been Providence Himself who just dropped it out of the sky and into my hands not more than fifteen minute ago."

"Ah! Very good, Johnson! Very good! I'll take that right now!" There was even less doubt in my mind as to what this gen-teel member of the most noble of pedestrian art forms was about to place into my anxious hands, so I quickly snatched it from him, whirled about and stood right over that jolly sack of howling intellection, held it out at arm's length, and said triumphantly, "There you are, Doctor! Now just try to explain *that* one, if you can!"

He lay on his back for some moments panting and heaving and wiping the tears from his eyes. But then, when he realized what I was holding out for him to see, the perplexity and amaze-ment must have been too much for him, for he lunged at it like a starving feline about to devour its scurrying repast, tore open the brown envelope, took out the lett—

Tore open the brown envelope?!

"I knew it would come! Isn't that marvelous, Jeremy! Let me see—yes, you can tell from the postmark that it was indeed sent on the fourth, so it must have been misdirected, probably to that house the next street over. They really should do a better job around here of differentiating street names. Well, but why bother about that? With this money I can easily travel to Paris for a few weeks and still have enough left over for that leather-bound set of Heisenberg's complete works. I say, isn't that astounding, Jeremy?"

"Who's Jeremy?"

"Where's the tumbler?"

"Got my newspaper as well?"

"No."

"I am."

"Tumbler?"

"Well, how about the food coupons?"

"I thought your name was Roger."

"You don't need any more coupons!"

"Yes, that's right—didn't you see it?"

"I gave them all to Ms. Carter."

"He calls me Jeremy."

"Who?"

"Oh, you mean that glass thing."

"Why not? You can get butter for almost nothing."

"You know who—she just bought the house next door."

"I can't stand the name myself."

"So that was a tumbler—was it expensive?"

"Is she married?"

"You should be eating margarine!"

"Certainly not in pounds—but it's cost Jeremy a fair amount of aggravation."

"I don't think so."

"Well it's all your fault!"

"You must introduce me some time."

"She was rather startled when it smashed onto the pavement."

"I knew it!"

"And so was I."

"Tomorrow afternoon, perhaps?"

"We'll have to send a formal apology…"

"Why not! Meet you out front."

"Splendid."

"Maybe invite her to tea…"

"Four o'clock then?"

"Done!"

He stole away as inauspiciously as he had come. I threw myself back on the couch with the distinct intention of obliterating all thoughts of clarity and precision as quickly and completely as possible.

"I could go for a cup right now. How about you, Jeremy?"

"No thanks, Doctor. I think I need some rest."

"Yes, yes indeed, you rest my boy, and I'll put the kettle on." He started toward the kitchen but then paused at the threshold. "Now—don't move too far!"

I threw a pillow at his head, but he ducked and cackled and clattered his way to tea.

So now I am going to sleep. But before I do, I would ask anyone perusing this article to consider the outcome of such preposterous thoughts as this otherwise quite sensible professor has been upholding with all the stubbornness of a senile water buffalo. Things don't move! Just look around you. Look at the tables, chairs, walls, windows, books, picture hangings. Keep looking for a few moments, maybe a full minute. (Go ahead and use your watch—never mind him.) Did you see anything move? Hmmm? See anything shift position even one little bit? No, under ordinary circumstances, nothing moved. Not even you, except for your breathing. So I am laying here now saying this, and you are reading this, and time is passing. Yes, that is undeniable. But nonetheless, nothing is moving. If you just sat and sat in that chair holding this book, for say, fifteen years, your hair would go gray, the paper would get yellow, your eyesight would get a bit weaker, your breathing might become a little wheezy, the furniture would get dusty… We know all this. But nothing is moving, right? I mean, not like the pillow that I almost whacked that scoundrel with just now… Funny how we think of the future as a place. Even if we just sat still, we would go there. But no—is it the future? Or still the present? Would the past disappear? If so, where? Well, I'm sure we'll never know, since no one with any common sense or consideration for the opinion of his fellow human being is going to sit in a chair for fifteen years. No way. And why not? Because we have to move, really move. Arms, legs, head, chest, waist, buttocks, the whole contraption. And everything else would move, too. Somebody will sell the furniture, take a book, rearrange the pictures. That's right, *really* move things. None of this metaphysical stuff. Hmmm… So it does seem that everything is moving after all! But *my* way, not his. Yes… Yes! That's it! Well now, after this nap, I think I'll treat myself to a nice cold beer—from a new tumbler. I'll pour it vigorously and taste the delicious foam and cool liquid. Who cares even if it dribbles on the carpet. It is, after all, so rewarding—to be right!

The Highly Improbable Legend
of Lucas McClintock

The Highly Improbable Legend
of Lucas McClintock

I CANNOT UNDERSTAND why people still ask me to tell them Lucas stories. It always bewilders me. A few years ago, when Annie and I used to dine every evening at the Almost Horseshoe, it became something of a routine, a ritual even, for a couple of the younger townspeople to come over to our table while we were drinking our coffee and eating our pie and ask me to join them in the bar for a drink and a story. I always found it hard to refuse, especially since Annie would glare at me whenever I seemed the slightest bit reluctant. But I could never feel entirely comfortable about it. The stories themselves are curious enough, and I certainly hope that the most important details of the legend remain a part of Canoga County folklore for many generations to come. But why me? To begin with, I am not the most qualified person in the region to be telling Lucas McClintock anecdotes. I only actually saw the man once, when I was about seven years old, and it was from a fairly long distance away at that. And even though I did see something strange take place during those few brief moments, I cannot now quite believe all the details of it anymore myself. After you've seen something, and remember it again later, you can always find, if you think hard enough, other possible reasons and explanations

41

about what took place. Second of all, I'm not a good storyteller. This is a simple fact. I don't even like telling stories. There are so many details to remember, which I always forget; and people always want to get excited about what they hear, which they never do once I get involved in the narrative. At least, they don't get as excited as I do. But I cannot understand why I get excited either. After all, it's just a story; it's not really happening now. Then there is a third point, which is the all-important one: Barnabas is still alive. Many people have forgotten about that, but not me. Now I know for a fact that he spent several years with Lucas—he lived at that time only a half mile down the road from the McClintock farm, just near the Brison Fork—and that he was even with the man when he disappeared. But Barnabas is more clever than I am. He doesn't say anything to anybody, and so nobody ever says anything to him. So after all these years, the only way that anyone could realize that old Barney Crabshaw must have been friends with Lucas McClintock would be if they were to stop and consider how old Barney is, when Lucas supposedly lived, where Lucas supposedly lived, and where Barney was known to have lived. If anyone bothered to make all these calculations, and told their friends about it, I am sure that half the population of Tennessee would be storming the Crabshaw ranch in no time. But people don't seem to think of things like this, so it's not too likely to happen. Instead they ask me. And after I convince them that, yes, he was like that, and, yes, there are many other stories about the fellow, and yes, I will tell you one of them, then once again I get stuck. I must confess, some years ago it was a great

pleasure for me to sit back in my rocking chair by the fireside or
to sit over a good sour-mash whiskey in the Almost Horseshoe
and tell a few Lucas tales. But everything changes with time,
even me; and so now, whether I enjoy telling my story or not,
whether I begin my anecdote with enthusiasm or with marked
reluctance, whether I tell it to a perfect stranger, a new employee
on the farm, or my own grandchildren, I always find myself getting drawn in in the same old way. I start talking, and look at
the silent faces all around me, and then begin to describe the
gigantic oak tree near Bowman's Creek; and soon I'm picturing
it again inside my head, just like I did the first time I heard it,
and I get so far into my tale; then I forget some important details
and go back and put them in, and then when I get to the funny
part, I want to start laughing myself, and then I start feeling a
little tired, like I always do after I've been talking for a while, and
then suddenly I look—and there are all the faces still looking at
me and listening, some of them smiling, some of them dreaming,
others thinking it over, but all of them with eyes wide open, just
waiting to hear more and more. They look right at me, but it's not
really me they're looking at. No, it's Lucas McClintock. And this
makes me stop because, well, first of all I don't know where these
people really go to when they're staring like that and, second of
all, I don't quite know where I disappear to either while I'm telling the story. I wouldn't mind so much, except that it always tires
me out before I want to get tired out. But those faces just keep
watching; they keep looking and listening. I don't know how they
manage to do it without getting tired themselves. But the story is

so funny and strange that I suppose it makes up for my terrible manner of telling it... Oh well, there I go again. All this time has gone by and I still haven't been saying what I want to say. But that's how it is with me. At this point in my life I am just too exhausted to think precisely and coherently about any subject, no matter how strange that subject might be. Everything becomes the same after a while. Instead, I'm trying now to write everything down so that other people can read it when they want to, and even memorize parts of it and tell it to others that they might happen to meet. The latter idea is probably the best approach, because I won't be able to give you this whole legend in one neat chronological monologue from birth to death, world without end amen. I simply can't remember all the details in such an orderly way. Instead I'll just jot down each story, rumor or description about Lucas as I remember it, and then just hope that the final result is reasonably coherent. If at some future time I remember something important that I don't put down here, I'll add it on later as an appendix, or supplement, or something, and publish it separately. But let me caution every would-be reader right now: there may not be anymore tales forthcoming, so when you finish reading this, don't get stuck on the idea of expecting something else.

Now just by chance, I happened to end my introduction with that one word that I always start my story with—stuck. This is the essence of all the strange problems and misadventures that beset that hapless farmer from Canoga County. He always got stuck. Or rather, things always got stuck to him. It is certainly normal to get stuck once in a while. Sometimes we get stuck in a crowd of people, sometimes we get stuck on someone we're in love with, sometimes we get stuck on an arithmetic problem. Everybody gets stuck on something. But with Lucas it was different. He *really* got stuck. But again, I should probably say it the other way around: things really got stuck to him. You have no idea what stuck truly means until you hear how stuck Lucas was.

Oh, but now I'm getting stuck. So let me get started. I'll simply begin with the most well-known tale. It was a peaceful Saturday afternoon in early June in the year 19__. It already gets rather sultry in Tennessee at that time of year, but on this particular day there was only just enough heaviness in the air to make things a little slow and easy but still not too hot or uncomfortable. Lucas's wife, Mary, was in the kitchen baking pies and scrubbing the floor. She could hear from out in the front yard the short, high-pitched barks of Gyro and the happy laughter of her boy Todd. This made her happy as well, and she began singing to herself as she pulled the pies out of the oven and set them on the counter to cool. She remembered afterwards that while she was doing this she heard—or, at first, only thought she heard—the faint sound of a tree crashing to the ground somewhere in the hills. She thought this a little odd since she knew that there was no lumber industry in these parts and that all the forests were protected by the federal government. But she thought no more of it and opened all the kitchen windows to let in some cooler air.

And then she heard it again. Another crash, this time followed by the shouts of a couple of men. Their voices were too far away to hear clearly; but, as she stood still and listened, she heard the crashing and cracking noise become more and more continuous and more and more discernible. In fact, whatever it was she was listening to, it was making its way down the hill and through the forest in the direction of her home.

Mrs. McClintock began to feel a little bit frightened, yet she still did not panic. As often happens when we encounter something unusual or unexpected, she began to give herself reasonable explanations as to why she was hearing this strange noise and to tell herself that in any case there was no need to be concerned about it because there was no reason to expect anything to happen to her personally, and...

And another crash! Right in the clearing on the other side of the fence! She screamed and dropped the pie she was holding. It splattered all over the floor. Then she heard Todd scream and start crying. Gyro was yapping madly, and the chickens shrieked and cackled like they were being attacked. The crashing sound grew larger and louder and closer, and so did the shouts of several men and women. Mrs. McClintock could hear them clearly now: "You maniac!" "We ought to string you up!" "I'll throw a chicken at you!" "The sheriff's gonna hear about this!" But before the woman could run out to see what in the world was going on, she heard the picket fence groan and crack and shatter to pieces, and all the men and women scream and run off in all directions. The crashing sound grew louder and louder! It was coming right toward the house! The walls shook, the dishes and furniture rattled, two pots fell off the wall and clattered to the floor—and then a tremendous explosion burst right through the front wall! Windows smashed, bricks thudded on the roof, timbers creaked and split, Mrs. McClintock swooned and fell to her knees. But before she lost all consciousness, she was startled to hear the voice of her husband calling to her from the front room in a happy, excited tone: "Mary, Mary! Come quick! I must tell you about what I've just seen!"

Mary was both confused and relieved to hear his voice, and she stood up and rushed toward the front door terrified that something might have happened to him. But then, just before she stepped into the hallway, a new terror entered her heart. She stopped and closed her eyes. "No, no, please, it can't be," she said to herself. She gripped the handle on the door, slowly pushed it forward, leaned her head out into the hallway and opened her eyes. It was.

"Mary! Mary!" Lucas said with excitement. "I must tell you about this wonderful big oak tree I just saw up at Bowman Creek! You know how you like oak trees. Well…"

But Mary had covered her face with her hands and started to cry. "Oh, Lucas, what have you done now!"

Lucas scratched his head in bewilderment. He looked down and saw that his shirt and jeans were torn and covered with dirt and brambles. He hadn't noticed that until just now. Then he felt something poke him in the back. He hadn't noticed that before either.

There it was, protruding right through the front door and both front windows of the McClintock home—the gnarled roots of the enormous oak tree, caked with mud and entangled with bits of curtain, bed sheets and barbed wire. Cracked wood and broken glass lay everywhere. Lucas leaned out one of the side windows and looked into the front yard. The huge trunk extended from the front porch all the way out to the main road. The white picket fence, the clothesline and all the new wash, pieces of the chicken coop, a wheelbarrow, a stepladder—and even old Georgie Parker—were all caught up and entangled in the enormous spread of branches. The crowd was beginning to gather again. A few of them were helping old Georgie out of the tree, while a few others stared at Lucas without saying anything. Todd sat on the road in utter disbelief and held Gyro to his chest.

Lucas pulled his head inside the window and turned to face his sobbing wife. "Well, Mary," he said ruefully, "it certainly is a mess, isn't it."

I'm not going to give you too much time to ponder over that one just yet. While I still remember most of the details, let me set down the second most well-known Lucas story. This incident occurred the following October and, when it was all over, it brought everything and everyone to such a high-pitched momentum of fever and anger and frustration and you name it, that neither Lucas himself nor the people of Canoga County could remain the way they used to be ever again. But I'll come to that. What happened this other time was that Lucas had got himself all excited, in his usual cheery and uncompromising way, when Canoga County won the state baseball championship. Going into the bottom of the ninth they were still down by three runs, and even though Chester and Raymond got on base because of a Murtchison error, Canoga's two best hitters then struck out back to back, leaving Lucas and all the county fans in almost total despair. But somehow little Leroy Pooles hit one just over the second baseman's head to drive in one run, and then Sam Lacey finished everything by whacking the first pitch right into the Murtchison bullpen. Everyone in the Canoga stands roared out of their seats and onto the field and carried Sam away on their shoulders toward the center of town. Lucas, as I alluded to earlier, got more excited than everyone else put together, and he all but ran straight home to tell his Mary the good news. Along the way he stopped and shouted at every neighbor he saw, "We won! Canoga finally won!" and tried to explain in a few breathless words how it all happened. Now I know that Lucas himself admitted later on that he couldn't quite understand why all those neighbors had stared at him so strangely as he declared Canoga's triumphant moment. He remembered gesticulating wildly and talking so fast that the words hardly came out in the right sequence; he remembered feeling that he might have been a trifle rude to old Mrs. Curlbaum and the Hodson family when he told them about Leroy's tenacious hit; and he remembered that almost everyone he spoke to before he arrived at his own farm received his happy news with rather disappointing expressions, disappointing that is from Lucas's point of view. He noticed that for some reason they just didn't feel or understand what he was experiencing, even though he was trying his best to describe it to them in the most vivid way he knew how. In fact, most of the people he spoke to seemed a bit repelled by him and all but looked the other way as he spoke. So when he finally arrived home and saw Mary sitting on the front porch with Todd in her arms, he wasn't all that surprised when his first two or three exclamations of delight failed to stir his wife into a similar state of ecstasy; but he certainly was surprised when he saw her freeze in her rocking chair, lift Todd off her lap and place him on the floor, spring up out of her chair and rush down the stairs toward him with the most anxious and startled expression he had ever beheld on the face of his beloved. And he was even more surprised yet again when, as she got closer and closer to him, she began tearing at her hair and shouting, "Lucas Bartholomew McClintock! What in the name of Robert E. Lee are you and your crazy friends doing! Have you gone completely hog-mad!" Now it would be difficult for anyone to understand, if we just looked at this incident from Lucas's point of view, what it was that made his dear companion get so upset and horrified. So let me just back up the story by a few moments and describe it to you from Mary's perspective. There she was, rocking to and fro with her delightful little boy squirming in her lap and asking her countless questions about the trees and birds and clouds, when she heard several men shouting something like, "Hey Lucas! Come on now, stop! Lucas, look what you're doing!" All of their imprecations were seemingly to no avail, because as the group entered the clearing and approached the front gate, Mrs. McClintock witnessed the most bizarre spectacle she had ever seen (which was saying something). There was her excited

50

husband walking down the road with eyes wide open and arms waving this way and that, trying his best to say something to her, despite the fact that there was a baseball in his mouth. And what was even more strange was that the entire Canoga County baseball team—Sam Lacey, Chester Wills and all the rest—were all jammed up together in one long line right behind Lucas, with Sam himself pressed right up against her husband's back. They were all shouting at Lucas to let them go, but the unfortunate fellow was too absorbed in his own enthusiasm to notice that the subject of that enthusiasm was a lot closer to him than he expected!

Well, I am sure you can fully appreciate Mary's reaction now. But she was more upset than you or I would have been in the same circumstance because she had already been living with this problem of Lucas's for over three years. After she calmed down a bit, she shook her husband by the shoulders, popped the baseball out of his mouth (Sam's home-run ball) and helped untangle the heap of arms, legs, and uniforms that had all been dragged en masse almost half a mile by the overzealous farmer from Tennessee. A crowd of curious onlookers who had followed this strange parade stood together in small groups asking each other if what they saw was really true and pointing at Lucas as though he were a stranger phenomenon than Mount Rushmore. Poor Lucas was once again bewildered beyond explanation, and between apologizing to his wife and to the Canoga team, he all but forgot about their triumphant victory. And this was no doubt a blessing because, had he started describing Sam's glorious moment once more, the whole team would probably have shot right back at Lucas like so many iron filings to a magnetic bar.

I don't expect you to believe any of this. I hardly believe it myself. But there is really not much more I can say. Things got stuck to Lucas. Anything. All kinds of things. People, trees, houses, animals, books, water bottles. That's right. They got stuck right to him. It was always something he was excited about, or attached to, or fascinated by, or sometimes, even something that frightened him. There was a story going around for a long time that when Lucas came across a brown bear while he was hunting rabbits in the Wamopok Valley, he flew out of there like a cannonball and ran five miles without looking back all the way to Clover City. But when he entered the main street, all the towns-people fled from him as though he were a disembodied spec-tre; and it was only when the sheriff leveled his shotgun right at Lucas's head that he recognized the sensation of warm fur and rapid breathing against his back and shoulders. Yet like I say, that was only a rumor.

How did all of this come about, you might ask? Was it some kind of voodoo, or mass hallucination, or maybe just a healthy supply of that good old Tennessee sour mash? Well, no. None of these things. But nobody really knows how or why Lucas started experiencing this problem. Not even Lucas himself. In fact, for the longest time it was difficult for him to accept that there was a problem. Only when he saw over and over again the conse-quences of his excitement and—to use a word that I learned from some travelling doctor a few years back—"self-effacement" in the presence of things and people that particularly caught his fancy, did he see the need to do something about it. And do something he did. Although, funnily enough, when things started changing for the better for Lucas, a lot of people became disappointed. There was no more fun. No more excitement. A lot of things are only exciting when you talk about them later. While it's actually happening, most people just get mad, or scared, or both.

Now let me give you some more background. It all started just after Lucas and Mary bought their own farm six miles east of Clover City. The neighbors had noticed right away that this cheery young couple and their lovely little boy all seemed rather attached to each other—attached in a way that made other people a trifle uncomfortable. Lucas and Mary always went shopping together; Lucas and Mary always went to church together; Lucas and Mary always went everywhere together. Of course, to see a young couple spending all of their time with each other was nothing unusual. This is usually admired by many people and even envied by some. But there was something a bit odd here because Mary often seemed to be going where Lucas wanted to go even when she didn't really want to herself. There was that time, for instance, that Helen Maplewood was conversing with Mary at the Saturday market, and then Mary started walking away from her—backwards. She walked up the aisles and in and out crowds of people without looking over her shoulder until she bumped into her husband at the candy counter. "Mary, look at these!" Lucas exclaimed. "They're the most delicious thing I ever tasted. Try one now!" Even though it was obviously not her fault,

Mrs. Maplewood still never spoke to Mrs. McClintock again. And then there was the way they walked. They were always touching. No, I don't mean holding hands or arm in arm, although they did that too, no, I mean just touching, usually shoulder to shoulder. There was that episode many will never forget, especially Mr. Crothers, when the McClintocks knocked down the aforementioned gentleman and walked right over him without realizing for one minute what had happened until this same gentleman started assailing them with enough abuse to make even a public executioner blush with shame. Lucas couldn't remember anything except that he had been engrossed in telling his wife about a new tractor he was thinking of buying. But he could not deny the fact that his footprints were all over the good gentleman's grey trousers and white shirt and, needless to say, he apologized profusely and repaid the poor man for his misfortune.

Things got more peculiar still. People first started noticing that there was something definitely out of the ordinary on that first Thanksgiving the McClintocks spent in their new home. Lucas had paid a visit to his friend Cornelius, his closest neighbor, to borrow his carving knife. Just as he was walking out the door with it, he noticed Dorothy place her freshly-cooked turkey on the table and cried out with admiration, "Now, Dorothy, that is the most beautiful and succulent specimen I have ever set my eyes upon! I must congratulate you!" The woman smiled and concealed her proud feelings, and Lucas went off across the field to his own holiday meal. But a few minutes later, as Dorothy and Cornelius were setting the plates out on the table, they both gasped with astonishment as their delicious brown bird lifted itself right off the platter and sailed out the window. Cornelius dropped three plates on the floor and jumped out the window after it. He was just able to catch a glimpse of it in the twilight as it flew across the field and right through the McClintock's front window. He charged up the stairs and pushed open the door without even knocking. And there was his dear friend Lucas McClintock about to apply his very own carving knife to the breast of his long-awaited Thanksgiving dinner. Lucas had just been telling everyone at the table what a superb cook Dorothy was and, when the turkey had appeared through the window and slipped itself right under the knife, he was ready to start cutting it up and pass it out without a second thought. But that was only because Lucas hadn't noticed what was going on. As with every other incident, both previously and to come, he just didn't realize in his excited state of mind how attached he became to the things that affected him. Cornelius took back both the bird and the carving knife and didn't speak to Lucas again for a whole year. They almost made it up at Christmas time, but unfortunately Dorothy's culinary achievements aroused Mr. McClintock's admiration once again, and this time when Cornelius burst into the room, the delectable fowl was hanging by its drumstick from the excited jaws of Canoga County's most singular enthusiast.

This kind of circumstance plagued the McClintock household for a long time. Mary eventually had to plead with her husband almost to tears not to do any more of the family shopping, since he almost always came home with an assortment of utensils, cakes, ropes, wine openers, fishing tackle, or whatever else stirred his innocent heart, either draped around his neck and shoulders or bulging from the pockets of his shirt and trousers. The McClintocks only ever played bingo once at the community center and that was because Lucas was so excited and happy for old Mrs. Barker, who went away with over $5,000. Or so she thought. Sheriff Bloore followed a trail of twenty-dollar bills right to the McClintock's side entrance and collected the money without a fuss. At first he refused Lucas's offer of a glass of whiskey by the fire, but he changed his mind ten minutes later when he went back to the farm again to collect his revolver. The sheriff recalled that evening by the fire most vividly many years later, largely because of his surprise at Lucas's knowledge of firearms, but also because of his relief that the innocent young man's interest was only an intellectual one.

Then there was the time that Lucas went all the way to Memphis to have a new suit tailor-made for Easter Sunday (and for his son's birthday, which was only a few days prior). It certainly was a beauty, a three-piece pale grey suit, all wool and hand sewn, with special matching buttons and a silk lining; Lucas certainly struck a fine, handsome image on that Easter morning. He strutted about in front of the church as proud as a peacock, and nearly everyone in Canoga County who saw him that day made sure to compliment him on the beauty of the fit and the smartness of the design. I think something in their inborn instincts told them to compliment Mr. McClintock in this way, and indeed they were correct in doing so, for Lucas was so attached to his beautiful suit of clothes that for several months there were no incidents with other people's belongings whatsoever. But that hiatus came to an end the following September when, as Lucas stepped up to bat at the farmer's Labor Day softball game, Barney Crabshaw, who was catching for the opposing team, looked up at his friend and whispered, "Hey, Lucas, don't you think it's about time you took it off?" Lucas looked down at his treasured vestments and immediately concluded that since there were large holes in both knees and both elbows and that since there was the distinct odor of axle grease and gasoline all over the jacket and that since his matching silk tie had been chewed off by one of his stallions last week and that since the summer months had bleached vest, jacket and trousers the color of old parchment and that since his recent loss of weight frequently compelled him to walk around with one hand holding onto the seat of his pants and that since it was still rather hot these days, it probably was a good idea to take the advice of his faithful friend. While Lucas had been considering all of these things, he took three strikes right down the middle of the plate. This happened every time he went to bat in that game, but even that, along with the fact that his team lost by eight runs, did not bother Lucas so much as the realization that his beloved suit was no more. Besides, it took the winning team nearly two months to find the Labor Day trophy on Lucas's bookcase in the hallway.

And so it went. I must say that people were mostly kind to the McClintocks during these years of trial and embarrassment. There was very little gossip and very little wish either to put Lucas behind bars or to do any mischief to him or his family. Several men had even volunteered their time helping Lucas repair his house after the oak tree dilemma. People only felt it necessary to guard their own belongings when he was around and to maintain a more modest disposition in both conversation and activities, so as to avoid arousing any undue curiosity or interest. You see, Lucas was actually a very popular man. He was probably the most intelligent farmer in all of Tennessee. Local farmers often came by on Saturday mornings to get his advice on planting, harvesting, maintenance, or marketing. When they did come and see Lucas, though, he was frequently absorbed in his breakfast. This means that a person had to peel the morning newspaper off his face and chest in order to say hello, and then had to sit and carry on an intelligent conversation while enduring the sight of someone who was literally plastered with flapjacks and oatmeal. "Mary really knows how to make 'em," he used to say in a muffled voice.

No, there was not much gossip, but there was some. Most of it had to do with one of Lucas's most serious attachments—serious after his own peculiar style, that is. Once I tell you about it, you might even start gossiping yourself. Stories like this always get people going in one way or another. Lucas and Mary were most happy together, right through to the end. At no time did either partner harbor any secret desires to be with someone else. But of course, the nature of a couple's relationship does change over the years no matter what they do, and then there was this little difficulty that Mr. McClintock had. The young farmer was always personable to the young ladies of the town and liked to tease them or compliment them on their good looks. For a while Lucas was most fond of talking with Laura Mason whenever he bought feed or equipment at the big supply depot. Laura worked there now and then and was also well-educated in animal husbandry. She and Lucas always had things to talk about, and Lucas liked to give her chocolates that, by the way, she never thought of eating herself. Well, anyway, Mary McClintock fell asleep one night listening to her husband go on about Laura. "Yes," he said staring at the ceiling with his arms folded behind his head, "she'll make someone a mighty fine wife some day." Soon after Lucas put out the light, Mary felt him press up right against her side. She didn't mind, even though there wasn't a lot of room left on the bed, but fell right back to sleep again. However, sometime later she was awakened again, this time by some loud snoring. This by itself would not have roused her out of her slumber except that Lucas never snored. Lucas never... She sat right up in bed, turned on the light and I don't suppose I have to tell you further what she saw. She let out the most terrific shriek ever heard in all of Northern Tennessee. And a few moments later this was followed by the second most terrific shriek ever heard in Northern Tennessee, because Laura had no idea how she ended up in the McClintocks' bedroom either. Since so many of the neighbors were startled out of their dreams by all this commotion, there was no way of concealing these understandably embarrassing circumstances. Lucas gave Laura his overcoat to wear home, and Cornelius drove her back in his truck. Mary had to forgive him that time, but it did become more difficult for the poor woman. Four weeks later Todd's school teacher Grete turned up one morning sleeping as peaceful as a baby (she didn't snore) and when, two months after that, they had returned from a weekend visit to Mary's sister Ethel in Kentucky, and Lucas had been remarking how beautiful Ethel was, and Mary had turned down the bedspread and blankets for the evening, and had seen her sister lying there grinning dreamily, she not only passed out stone cold right on the spot, but was laid up in bed herself for eight days with a high fever. Lucas's concern for his beloved was so great that he had trouble keeping the thermometers out of his own mouth and also so great that these incidents ceased completely. They did not speak about it again to each other, but Mary realized that silence itself sometimes has a lot to say, especially since she never afterwards experienced much difficulty getting stuck to her husband's shoulder. She was able to move more freely, but it made her uncomfortable.

I should probably describe to you now the one time I saw Lucas McClintock myself. I haven't related this memory of mine too often, so it may seem a bit hazy in the telling. In fact, at the time I never considered what I was seeing to be anything of unusual significance. My daddy never spoke much about Lucas, and I don't remember having heard much about him either while I was growing up. But when the legend really started to grow some twenty years back, it made me think about it again, and now I realize just how strange that incident was. My description of it all has to be a bit sketchy. Whenever we think back to memories from long ago, there are always big gaps left out. It's sort of like a badly edited film that jumps suddenly from one scene to the next or a long novel with dozens of pages torn out. I don't know why our memory gets that way, but I think I still remember enough to give a coherent story. I remember coming out of the barber shop just after getting a haircut. The air was cool around my ears, and I was eating a lollipop—cherry, I think it was. I was with my daddy, and he had stopped on the avenue to have a talk with somebody. I can't remember who. But I do remember that while I stood there waiting for him to finish, I noticed a group of men and women come out of the grocery store across the street. One of them stood out from the rest. He wasn't taller or stronger looking than the other men, but he seemed somehow happier and, what was more significant, the others seemed to be following after him. He walked a little ways down the street and then stopped. The others grouped around him in a sort of semi-circle. My daddy and his friend noticed them just then as well, and I remember the friend saying, "What's McClintock up to now?" Lucas was explaining something to the small crowd, and as he went on, the crowd grew more and more excited about what he was saying. His voice seemed to grow louder (or may-be not, maybe I just started hearing him better); he laughed a couple of times and—something I could never understand—he kept pointing up at the sky. Whenever he did this a few of his listeners would look up for a few moments. Gradually the crowd got larger, and soon there were so many people around him, the only thing I could see was the occasional pointing of that finger above the heads of the others. After a while my daddy took me by the hand and we started to walk away. But I kept watching as we walked, and soon I saw Lucas break through the crowd and walk across the street. And then everyone else went right after him. And that was what was really remarkable because, when they started milling around him again, he broke through the crowd once more and walked over to his car. Everybody else did the same. I don't know how many times that happened, or if perhaps the crowd had to drive all the way home with him (though I wouldn't be surprised). The last picture that sticks in my mind is Lucas McClintock with one hand on the door of his vehicle and some of those men and women reaching out to touch him and say something to him. I bet it was something like, "Let us go, Lucas!"

There are a few other amusing Lucas anecdotes, but I've given you the most important ones. What remains is to tell you what happened to him after the episode with the Canoga County baseball team, because that was really the limit, both for Mrs. McClintock and the people of Clover City. Somehow Lucas had to be persuaded either to stop getting so excited about all the events that happened around him (most of which weren't so important anyway) or at least to find some way of not getting so stuck. Mary had pondered over a possible solution to this for several months, usually after watching another fresh pecan pie go flying out the window or after struggling with Lucas to help get the console radio off his chest. But she never came up with anything really practical. Yet that night after all the celebrating was over and both Sam and Lucas had staggered off to bed good and drunk, Mary and Barney sat out on the front porch and talked through all the possible methods that Lucas could use to cure himself. And then, Barney had it.

"You know, Mary, we've been thinking about this all in the wrong way."

"I know that, Barney. That's why we haven't found an answer yet."

"But now I realize what we have to do."

"Barney, don't you dare suggest that we put him down in that cave. That sheriff has some of the craziest ideas I ever heard—'Well, Mary, bats can't see, you know'—and besides, he just wants to save his reputation..."

"No, no, no, Mary. Nothing like that. But it's so simple; I'm amazed that I never thought of it before." And Mr. Crabshaw explained to Mrs. McClintock the solution that irrevocably changed not only her husband's life but her own as well and, in an indirect way, everyone else's in Canoga County.

When Lucas first had it explained to him, he could not comprehend its significance.

"Get stuck to myself! What does it even mean?"

"It doesn't matter what it means, Lucas. It's not a question of meaning. It's a question of doing. You're stuck; you want to get unstuck. That's all."

"So what do I do, then?"

"Whenever you feel yourself starting to get stuck on something, get stuck on yourself instead. Turn it around and think of yourself."

"What will that do?"

I think for a moment Barney got a little stuck in his impatience. "Don't you see!? All kinds of things are getting stuck to you now. But if you just think of you, remember you, then at the very worst you'll only get stuck on yourself. And you're already you, so everything will be all right."

"But what will happen to everything else? Won't it all go away?"

"Where? You're the one who's been going away! Everything else will just stay where it's always been."

Lucas didn't believe any of this, but he tried anyway. He had to try it, really, because Mary was beginning to allude to a "long vacation" with Ethel and "maybe farming isn't my style of living."

In the beginning it went well. Every time Lucas found himself starting to get excited over something, he thought of himself instead, and the thing that had started to attract him never quite stuck as before. Mary's first memories of his success with this refer back to the new 24-piece set of china she bought at Ebenezer Kidwell's auction. She had set it all out on the dining table one afternoon for some of her friends to see, when Lucas unexpectedly came in from the fields. "What a beautiful set, my love! Look at that soup tureen!..." No sooner had he said this than it flipped right off the table and spun toward him like a 40-yard field goal. Mary gasped and was about to yell at him to catch it, when it suddenly froze right in midair and dropped to the floor with a gentle crack. It only broke into three big pieces, but Mary wasn't looking at it anyway. She was more impressed by the sight of her usually excitable spouse standing in the middle of the room with his hands in his pockets and a gentle smile on his face. So it was possible. And difficult. Over the next several months Lucas had many fits and starts with his new exercise (in all, his wife lost two cake plates and a coffee cup), and after a while he concluded that it was necessary to do something to keep reminding himself to get stuck on himself and not anything else. For a time he tried jabbing himself in the cheek with his index finger every couple of hours; but one night he accidently poked himself in the eye and got so upset about it that both Dr. Tatum and Dr. Freemickle (Lucas's specialist in Memphis) found themselves on the doorstep of the McClintock farm at one o'clock in the morning—and Tatum was even in his longjohns. Eventually he found a more tame way of reminding himself, simply by doing everything a little slowly and a little more deliberately than he was ever accustomed to.

The effect was miraculous. After about a year nothing ever got stuck to Lucas again. Now of course, after I've told you about all the problems and trials he'd been through, it does seem miraculous that he never got stuck anymore. But on the other hand most people found it difficult to see "nothing" as being something miraculous. Because then Lucas seemed just as normal as anyone else. There was no longer anything special about him. I am not sure I can convey my meaning to you so clearly, so let me quote what Barney said about his friend a year after the "cure" took place:

"Yes, it was a miracle, a veritable miracle. Here was a man whom people were so accustomed to seeing weighed down like a burro with pots, pans and you name it, or completely submerged in the story he was trying to get out of his mouth to you, calmly going about his life like every little second was a county fair. I remember walking up the drive one morning and seeing Lucas rocking back and forth on his front porch. When he saw me, he stood up and walked down the steps to greet me. I saw the man. A man standing there in work boots, black bandana and wide-brim hat, his red and white two-story house behind him, his little dog sitting obediently at his feet, the daffodils nodding in the breeze, the trees and furniture and chickens and everything else all perfectly in their own place going about their own business. Everything being what it should be. Especially Lucas. Especially Lucas..."

It was a real event for a while for the people of Clover City to behold Lucas McClintock pick up a glass of beer in his hand and drink it, or to see him examine a rack of spades and picks in a hardware store and then choose the one he liked best. It was all so simple that people were really amazed. But like I say, after a time it ceased to be interesting. Lucas looked the way everybody else looked. He was no longer someone worth watching out for or worrying about, anymore than the rest of us are. It was said that he continued on in Canoga County for another two years, but when their second child arrived, he and Mary moved up to Kentucky and bought a ranch not far from Ethel and her husband. Lucas eventually became an expert horse breeder and accumulated quite a sum of money. I suppose he ended his days there and was buried on the ranch somewhere.

I say "I suppose" because no one knows for sure what happened to him. Barney used to visit the McClintocks now and then in later years, and he used to say that Lucas got so unstuck that he simply disappeared. "There was nothing to hold him back," Barney used to say, "Nothing to hold him back." There was a crazy story going around for a while that on a trip to the Appalachians, Lucas got so excited over seeing a particular mountain peak that he made like Mohamed and the whole monstrosity fell right on top of him. But it is human nature to think that people must end up the way they started out. No, I think Barney's account is closer to the truth. And that ties in with the other rumor about why Lucas went up to Kentucky in the first place. Like I said, he become so unstuck as to be almost invisible around Clover City. He would go to the bank or one of the stores on Main Street, and he was so quiet and self-contained that people hardly knew he was there. But once they did catch sight of him, they suddenly got filled with this strange curiosity about what was going on and why things were so different. "Hey, Lucas—look at that!" someone would say, throwing a bottle or tomato or bag of candy into the air, expecting at the next instant that it would go flying full tilt at its fascinated target. Instead, it just became someone else's mess to clean up. But people were undaunted. They would follow him out into the street and try to look in his eyes or watch the way he walked. They would shout, or poke him on the arm, or stand in his way. Some of them probably hoped to go flying around uncontrollably like that famous baseball team, while others just wanted to know how he did it. But Lucas would never say much, no matter how big a crowd he had around him. Only once in a while would he point up at the sky, and tell everybody, "Just a few feet up, there's all of that space. Just air. Nothing can touch you there. Just a few feet up." I never understood that one. The first time I heard that, I jumped up and down a few times. Of course, I always came down. Who doesn't.

Well, I'm sorry, but that's all. The memory of Lucas McClintock carries on in these parts of Tennessee and in years to come maybe the whole nation will be talking about him. The most important lesson that I personally get out of telling these stories is the understanding that a normal everyday existence is the best one of all. I suppose most of us should be relieved that we didn't have to go through the turmoil of getting stuck the way Lucas did to find this out. There was a time in my life when I thought more about this cure that he used—the method of getting stuck on yourself. I thought about it especially when I noticed myself getting drawn into my storytelling, like I told you before. But I couldn't find a way to do it. I can only conclude that since I'm not nearly as stuck as Lucas was that it's not something to worry about. Besides, I'm not interested in disappearing. A man my age begins to grow too fond of things, you know. Why there's my house, and Annie, and my pension, and the Almost Horseshoe and all my friends, and the baseball games. Those things are all a part of me. You might even say I am those things.

So for me to get unstuck wouldn't make any sense. Not when I already know who I am.

Ho Li

Ho Li

H O LI WAS A SCULPTOR. He lived in a bamboo hut by the river bank and carved wooden figures all day long. Merchants waved to him as they floated by. Sometimes they stopped and purchased his statues or traded for them with fish and rice. They revered this gentle old man with his calm blue eyes and time-worn face. Yes, that face—a face creased with truth and carved in wisdom. A face that gave the image of the beholder as did the rippling waters of the river. He sat cross-legged with blocks of sandalwood in his lap; a small fire smoked quietly by his side with several cutting blades stuck among the cinders. He would take one of them and open the block's eyes, and stroke it until it smiled and posed and beckoned to the fishermen with strident song. What was solid and indifferent became in his leather hands a fragile twig of feeling. The statues danced like little trees before his hut, suspended on the present.

Suspended... A statue is always present. Look, and look again, and it is always calling you, or brushing you aside for its larger purpose, or seeing what we all would wish to see. It always keeps the secret. Crack it open, smash it to fragments, burn it down to hot dust: its emptiness will still beckon you, or leave you suspended.

The young fisherman watched the wood block and watched the sage's hands. He could hear the other sailors singing on the river as he wafted the scent of sizzling fish in the pan. The blue twilight air was warm like the center of a candle flame. Ho Li cut the soft wood. Shavings clung to his hairy arms or dropped silently in his cloak. He ripped lines in the wooden face, not unlike his own. He cleaned away some fragrant shards and left an attentive ear. Soon a chin and lips emerged and slightly stirred as though about to speak. A sharp nose and sunken cheeks appeared. Then two cupped hollows began to see. The fisherman handed him a plate of fish, and Ho Li gave him the wooden head in return.

The young man gazed in wonder. "But this is your face!"

The sage ate his meal without speaking, but peered intently at the youth.

"How is it done?"

"By creating nothing."

"Nothing?"

"The wood is the wood. The face is the nothing that surrounds it."

"But no. If I scrape this off, then there is nothing. Really nothing."

The fisherman pulled out his long blade, stood the head on a flat stone, and with one broad stroke chopped away the Master's work. He tossed the face into the fire and held up the remaining piece between his thumb and index finger. He looked at Ho Li and smiled curtly. The sage responded with a like expression. This made the young man angry. Ho Li then looked angry too. The fisherman suddenly became frightened and saw an ancient visage seized with terror. He sprang up and raised his knife, as though to plunge it in the old man's heart, and saw that he was about to kill a murderer.

For many years the Emperor of China preserved under a glass dome the lacquered figurine that the old hermit by the river bank had given him. When the servant had first brought it to him in his dining hall, there was a small note tied to one of the legs with the words: "To what must we all yield?" The Emperor did not understand this, but because it was a message from so revered a subject, he restrained his first angry impulse and let the statue remain on his writing desk. As the months passed, he would often set down his quill amid the bother of the day to regard the figure and its curious details. What a strange posture this warrior held, if indeed a warrior. Was he lunging to attack? Or bracing to receive a horrendous blow? Or perhaps he was about to flee? The knife, oddly clutched in a confusion of fingers, as though urgently seeking the proper grasp for the moment. But which grasp? To slash his foe, parry an imminent danger? But no, he could well be about to relax his limbs and sheath his weapon. Or now, as the Emperor looked again, maybe he will turn the blade on his own exposed breast. And that face.

Horror? Anger? But no again, perhaps those tense muscles were just about to melt into the clearest peace. These and similar reflections turned each time he lingered over this companion to his daily toil. And as months became years, the Emperor gradually surrendered any attempt to settle the figure into one posture or emotion, concluding rather that this magical creation was at once all chaos, all intention, all repose, the inner dance of heart and mind, stretched across the span of a life, here compressed into a vibrant, all-embracing present.

And so often in these moments, he would turn about in his hand the other object that had accompanied the statue, a small wooden cube with one side smoother than the rest, which the Emperor would idly stroke with his fingertip.

Orias

Orias

THEN THERE CAME one called Orias, who stepped out of his abode as the first halo of light appeared in the East; and he was young, and confident as the morning air he breathed. And he was girded round with sword and dagger, and bore a shield of gleaming bronze upon his back, and gold bracelets on his wrists and ankles. His helmet was of burnished steel, and his face was fair as the sunlit sky; and he could speak with melody so fine, and intonation so clear, and aspect so wise and cunning, that it seemed to all who heard him as though the knowledge of all ages passed from his mind to his lips like the dancing fountains on Parnassus. He walked out into the morning, and the sleep and dreams of his evening succor were no more, but vanished from the fire of the day; and he did scan the valleys and the hills, and did set out upon the western road with iron step and blazing eagerness. For it was the will of the young Orias to encounter One who was a blight upon the kingdom, and who did goad the privileged and the weak alike to argue power for the land and to wage incessant combat until death itself gave answer to the victor.

And the armored youth walked clear and angry for many miles; and he would wield his heavy sword against the squirrels

and robins and low-hanging branches and fright them away into
their lairs, so that the One would see the earnestness of he who
was the worthy issue of kings and hope of all the kingdom.

And away along the road before him Orias saw the speck
of one who moved toward him with strident motion. And the
young warrior did fasten on his burnished helm and strap on his
blazing shield, and unsheathe his sword and cunning dagger; and
he raised his mighty arms straight into the air. And as the figure
grew larger and came closer, Orias saw it was a man of many
years who led an old brown horse laden with sacks and a cask of
wine. And Orias did stand in the way before him and called to
him thus:

"If you are friend or one inclined to battle, stand and behold
the idol of kings: for I am he, Orias, who seeks the One attending
our ire, and who stands a brazen foe to all our kingdom."

And the old merchant wondered at the sight of such a youth;
but he meekly bowed his head and replied, "Forgive me, young
lord, but I know him not. And now I would fain pass by and
continue on my journey before the sun be too high in the open
sky. Pray, let me pass."

But Orias would not let the merchant pass, but pressed him
further with his high-flown words, "Surely you have seen the One
I seek; or maybe even now you bring these goods to him so that
his strength shall wax stronger than my own. But this you shall
not do." And with one stroke of his mighty sword Orias beheaded
the old man's animal and removed the sacks and the cask from
its bleeding body. And the merchant wailed and beat the youth

with his little withered fists; but Orias grasped him by the tunic and with one arm hurled him against a tree. And thereunder the old man lay half-dead and weeping, and several leaves fell from the tree onto his shaking limbs.

So Orias continued on his journey, now and then refreshing himself from the goods he had removed from his first adversary.

And a little farther on he saw another distant speck along the road that moved toward him with strident motion. And soon Orias beheld an old woman hobbling slowly on her way with a gnarled club to support her weary frame and a young child strapped to her back, who laughed and giggled and played with the wisps of her grey hair. And Orias did stand in the way before her and called to her thus:

"Know, you wandering ancient, that I am Orias, the idol of kings, who seeks the One who would destroy our kingdom. Stand forth and tell me who you are, and who be this child that you bear upon your back."

And the woman did wonder at the sight of such a fierce and majestic youth, but she did smile and replied with tender words, "I go a journey into town, and follow after my husband as quickly as my strength allows me. And there will we sell our wares and furnish our home to make ready for the arrival of our son, whose child you behold a happy burden on my aged frame."

But Orias cried forth and said, "Such fortune only comes to one who dares! For now I see that your son is the One I seek, and that the evil man I halted on the road surely bore the goods that would make his strength wax stronger than my own. But now I have his child, and will prevent it from growing in stature lest it become the kinsman of his father and certain death to our land."

And saying this Orias took the laughing baby by the hair and pierced it through with his cunning dagger, then hurled the body away into a ditch. And then the woman shrieked horribly, and she fell upon the earth and screamed through her tears, "Surely my sorrow has pierced me as sharply as your vile blade has pierced my helpless one. Now must you kill me as well, else shall the knives of remorse dig deep into my breast for many days."

But Orias laughed and would not kill the woman. "Yet must you live until your son appears to taste the judgment of my mighty steel. For I am he who must destroy the One who imperils the helpless of our kingdom."

So Orias continued on his journey, and was fed with power and confidence by the deeds he had so far committed.

And a little farther on he saw another distant speck along the road that moved toward him with strident motion. And soon Orias saw it was a young man of as many years as he himself possessed; and this young man carried a sack across his shoulder and a polished staff in his hand. And when he saw Orias, he stopped and put down his sack, and raised his arm and called to him, "Hail to you, traveler! Have you passed along your way an old man and his burden and an old woman and her burden? For I travel after them and would fain be certain of their safe journey."

But Orias stood and raised his weapons over his head once again and cried out, "Oh Evil One, who would destroy this kingdom of my fathers and persuade every knee to crook itself in blind submission to your will, know that it is Orias who stands before you, and that the child of your flesh and blood has perished by this blade and that the parents of your fated life have been subdued by my ire. And now must you yourself encounter me, and pay for your insolence."

The young man stared as if possessed, and grew white with fear and anger; and with trembling voice and streaming eyes he addressed Orias thus, "Have you, a man of youth and armor, destroyed a helpless child and subdued the helpless offspring of old age in hope of thwarting me or any other who claimed to be an enemy of your land? Wicked! Wicked beyond words is your bestial ardor! And since I am not girded as yourself, I can do naught but bend my neck before your cowardly blade, and trust that the gods will grant me the vengeance I cannot myself achieve." And so saying he knelt before the brazen warrior and awaited the stroke of his brutal blade.

But then it happened that a whispering spark ignited itself in the breast of Orias, and in an instant he blazed with sorrow, and realized the fiendish errors of his deeds. And he dropped his sword and dagger and shield, and bowing his head before the young traveler, spoke to him thus, "No words are adequate to describe the terrors of my foolish heart! Now let me but kneel before you and you extract the service I may render to help repay this horrible crime."

But the young man smiled at his opportunity and said, "Such humbleness of manner could fool a man less wary than myself;

but as I know the ways of men like you, I need no further service than your submission." And so saying he raised his polished staff and struck Orias full upon the forehead. And Orias groaned and fell and covered his arms about his head; and the young man continued to beat him until he was still and senseless with the pain. Then the traveler took up the sword and dagger and shield and walked on to find his child and his unhappy parents.

After a time Orias rose and staggered along the road. His eyes and mouth bled, his body was bruised, and his vision was blurred and dizzy. Yet a little farther on he saw another distant speck along the road that moved toward him slowly and unsteadily. And it was then that Orias knew that the strident motion he had previously beheld belonged not to those he had encountered but to his own impetuous heart.

And soon Orias saw another young man leaning against a tree bleeding as well. And Orias came and stood before him and said, "Pray, tell me, friend, what mishap have you encountered, that I may help you in your pain. For I am called Orias, and as you can witness, I am no stranger to this, your misfortune."

And the young man smiled and thanked him, and fell into his arms. And when Orias had laid him by the road, the young man spoke and said, "I thank you for your compassion, good friend. A robber has beaten me and taken my goods, and I have nothing now but these rags and this, my staff. Help me if you can." And Orias made as if to answer this unfortunate soul, when suddenly there came a rush of steps behind him, and a cry of several voices; and then the traveler in rags sprang up, and seized his club, and said, "Yet are we fortunate today to find a pretty boy adorned with so many beautiful trinkets. Come, let us take our fill." And so saying he and his three companions, who had been concealed behind the trees and bushes, took up their staffs and beat Orias senseless once again. And they removed his burnished helmet and his bracelets of gold and the other jewels upon his fingers, and they left him still and bleeding by the tree.

After a time Orias rose and staggered along the road; but he fell again. Yet he arose again and came upon a pond of cool water and a tree of sweet fruit; and he did rest and gather up his strength. And then he continued on his way.

And a little farther on he saw another distant speck along the road. And as he moved toward it, he saw it was a beautiful young maiden with golden hair who carried a basket filled with flowers and cakes and who was travelling along the road in the same direction as himself. And when he came upon her she was frightened, and she stared at him with uncertain eyes. But he smiled and said, "Surely must you fear the wolf, and the pale light of the hideous moon. But I am one who bears the name Orias; and if there is any service I can render you, fair maid, only name it and it is done."

But the maiden smiled and said to him, "I fear not for the safety of my person, which I am certain the gods at all times protect, but for the wounds upon your head and face. Surely you have been wrongfully abused and need the succor of another's hand." And so saying she did press her warm hands against his face; and Orias did feel the softness of her cheek, and the perfume of her hair, and the song of her voice; and he was flushed with joy. "How it could be, dear girl, that you could bear a heart so unselfish as to fear for my pain and not your own, I know not. But do know that I love you and wish to be your friend and husband, and treat you as you most deserve." And the maiden blushed and smiled sweetly, and Orias took her hand and held it to his heart.

And now they two did walk along the road together; and the fire of joy inside Orias burned brighter than the ardor of his morning courage. And he no longer feared the One who would destroy the land, but walked on fearlessly, eager to embrace that terror and persuade it to his happiness.

And a little farther on they saw another distant speck along the road. And as they drew nearer they beheld it was a man with tousled hair and swarthy face who held a little boy roughly by the hand. And this wild man did curse and swear at the little child with besotted anger, and did beat him about the head and back with his heavy open palm. And when Orias saw this, he at once sprang between the child and the man and addressed the rude aggressor thus, "Perhaps you find justice or pleasure in the easy abuse of gentle natures; but know, sir, that I can well assure you of your folly, and beg you to cease a present need that will soon become a bitter worm in your heart. I am a foolish man that was given the name Orias and I would gladly help you end this wayward hate."

The little boy was silent and stared at Orias with wide blue eyes that welled and dropped a stream of tears down his cheeks and lips. But the wild man, his father, did flush with further rage and grasped Orias by the tunic; and with his huge red fist he struck the young man full in the face.

And Orias shouted and stumbled to his knees; but then the fire of revenge, new-mingled with his passionate love, blazed brighter in his heart than the whitest star, and he drew himself up and seized the wild man by the hair and beat him until he groaned and fell bleeding to the earth.

And the little boy shrieked and sobbed wildly, and threw his arms about his father's neck and kissed his many wounds. Then he turned and ran at Orias' legs and kicked him about the ankles and cursed him thus, "You beast! If you have killed my father, I will surely find the men to end your wretched life!" And he wept more bitterly than before.

And Orias was sorry for his misdeed and could not plead for good intentions now destroyed. And his wife did also berate him and took him by the arm and said, "We must depart quickly, or other men will hear the boy and come to kill us both."

And they two departed on the road again, and the woman railed and argued hot words against her husband's foolishness. And every word was like a living wasp within his breast.

A little farther on they saw another distant speck along the road. And as each traveler drew nearer to the other, the woman saw it was a handsome man of sorrowful countenance who bore a sack across his shoulder and leaned in weariness upon his polished staff. The handsome man saw the beautiful woman and was joyful with the sight; but then he saw her companion, and hate blazed up into his heart again. And Orias saw it was the man whose child he had killed and whose parents he had humiliated. And he was heavy with his shame and could not speak to either man or woman.

And the woman said, "Unhappy man, we know not of another's joy or pain, but if there is a service that I or my husband Orias can render you, but only name it and it is done."

And the unhappy man's sorrow increased the more; and he said to the beautiful woman, "How like unto my own late wife are you, sweet friend. Once I was happy like yourself, but this, your husband, did destroy my happiness; now my wife has perished from sorrow, and surely such a fate shall soon envelop me as well." And he described to her the cruel encounters of long ago.

The woman was horrified and said to her husband, "Is it thus?"

And he replied but, "Yes".

And she did take the unhappy traveler by the hand and said, "It is impossible for me to be companion to such a fool and coward as this. For now I see the error of my generosity and would wish to cast away affection undeserved. Let me but go with you, kind friend, and together shall we kiss away the poison from our lives and greet the dawn with new unwonted promise."

And so saying she departed back along the way from whence she and Orias had come with her new lover; and Orias saw them not again.

And so he continued on his way, and the emptiness of the open sky was like the emptiness in his weary heart. And at times the doves of happiness that fluttered with remembrance of his joy congealed into the wasps and hornets of regret. And then the feelings in his breast would begin to spread further and further away, like the fleeting clouds that gain the rising air.

And a little farther on he saw another distant speck along the road. And as it grew larger, he knew not if it moved toward him or he toward it, or whether the present hour merely gave birth to new caprices. But soon he saw it was crowd of angry men who stood beside a pile of stones; and before them stood the little boy with tears in his eyes and his unhappy father with bandages about his head. And the little boy did point at Orias and say, "It is he, the fiend that calls itself Orias." And so hearing this, the angry men took up the stones into their hands and began to hurl them at Orias. And Orias threw his arms about his head and turned his back toward the ragged missiles; and wickedly they struck him all about his body like iron rain. And soon Orias fell upon the ground, and the stones pounded down upon him; and then he remembered nothing.

But later he awoke, and felt the heavy burden of the rocks; and they weighed so hard upon him that he struggled for air to enter into his mouth and nose. Then he heard the sound of footsteps, and then the sound of clattering rocks, and the pressure lifted from his weary chest. And he looked up and beheld a man who smiled down on him. And this man undid the tunic of Orias and pulled it off; and then he unlaced the boots of Orias and pulled them off as well; and did the same with his trousers and underclothing. And he put the clothes into a sack, and tossed it over his shoulder, and smiled at Orias as he walked away.

And soon it was dark, and the air was cold with wind and rain. And Orias departed on the way again; and he was naked and full of pain, and the water and the rain did cut into his trembling flesh.

And a little farther on he saw a distant speck of light along the road. And soon this light grew into a shimmering cocoon, and grew and grew again until it was a shining pillar that thrust itself into the blackened sky. And Orias fell upon his knees and hands and gazed into this whirling tower of light. And soon he saw that within it stood a giant man, as large as the largest mountain. And this man was girded about the waist with a belt of gold; and from this belt there hung a giant silver axe, with blade as sharp as would split a single hair; and in his left hand he held an enormous shield of hammered iron; and in his right hand he held a sword of polished steel that would cleave an oaken forest as if it were but summer grass. And this man had eyes of fire, and enormous wings upon his back; and when he spoke, it was as though the cracking thunder knew the gift of tongues. And it was thus that he addressed the naked one before him:

"The hour is ripe for encounter. As weeds before the curling scythe, so too are you before this unsheathéd blade. And thus the withered husk departs along the wind; and thus the choking seed may suck the crystal rain."

And so saying he drew up the mountain of his arm that held his unyielding blade and prepared to crash it down upon the object of his fury. But the naked one did cower into a little ball and called out with burbling words thus:

"If there be any mercy in the whistling storms, or if any tenderness abide among the silent sparkle of evening, then consider, O terrible One, that some time I had thought to make my slave, consider how my shriveled existence is but the plaything of the day and the indifference of the night. And if your heart be anything as large as is your shield, then find within it some unneeded fealty toward my worthless living."

But the angel did not lower his mighty arm, but instead stretched it forth before him and, pointing with his gleaming sword, he said: "Behold the One we both do seek. For it is he you have subdued as you did wish and he that I will now disperse into the nothing air."

And the little naked one turned about and looked back along the road he had traversed. And suddenly there sprang up from out this road an enormous Serpent of wicked tongue and hideous eye that coiled and crooked itself as though to strike. And this Serpent was girded round with spikes like sword and dagger, and its back was as of gleaming bronze, and its coils were wreathed with bracelets of gold, and its triangular head was as of burnished steel. And Lo! the Serpent was Orias.

And the little one trembled as he beheld this terrible vision. But yet he did not look away, but gazed and gazed more bravely at the fiend. And he beheld that on its polished scales there stood the fire of his morning insolence, and the arrogance of his callous words, and the cruelty of his cunning knife, and the blaze of his wanton anger, and the lust of his passion, and the rudeness of his justice, and all the bees and hornets of his breast. And as it swayed and rippled before him, the thunder of the angel's sword crashed down upon its skull, and blood as black as ink disgorged itself upon the wind.

And then the rain poured forth in crystal showers upon the naked boy. And soon the mud about his feet and ankles did suck him down into the earth; and then the morning beams of heaven made warm the silent ooze. And there sprang forth a bush of many branches that quickly burst with many crimson buds. And like the tender lids of infant eyes uncap themselves unto the precious day, these buds did open and kiss the dreamy air; and million roses sighed their perfume on the temperate breeze; and their fragrance swirled into an ether child that sought at once his cousin sunbeams, to tease them with his joy.

The Necklace

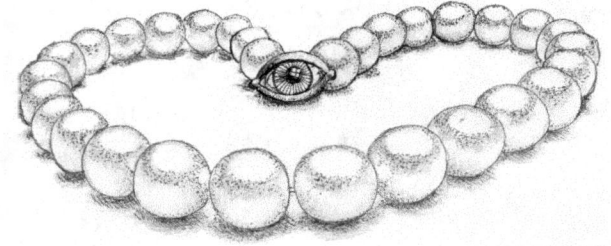

The Necklace

ONCE A YOUNG MAIDEN wandered along a windy road; and she wandered in the meadows warm with dew and yellow flowers; and she was unhappy. For she had loved someone and he had loved her; and then he was no more. He went away, and his love went with him; but her love did not go away. And she wandered long and far, and searched for him. Deep in the forest she came upon a sparkling fountain, whose crystal jet shimmered in the sun like a pillar of light. And her loving heart was like this fountain, and her shimmering jet of love burned, and rose from her loins, and passed through her wounded heart, and welled up into her tearful eyes. And the wind sighed and sprinkled water on her brow; and she sighed and sprinkled tears upon the earth.

And she wandered still, and never slept by day or by night. And the fire in her breast was the only light she possessed in a world of darkness. She would call out her lover's name, and he would not answer; and she would call again, and again the silent groves replied with but a deeper hint of her loneliness and her loving fire. And she remembered him, and remembered the days when they would walk and laugh, and call the world by names of their own choosing, and tell each other secrets only shared by the bees and the gentle wind. And she remembered his eyes, and soft voice, and wavy hair, and patient hands; and she would weep and weep again whenever she remembered. And she would close her eyes and lean upon a bough, and taste again his kiss, and drink it deep into her heart, until the fire burned as though her heart would die for longing. And then she would open her eyes again, and see the soft leaves flicker on the trees, and see the shy fawn and the laughing bird; and she knew again that she was alone. And so she would weep.

She walked for many months, and loved not the world, but loved her fire and her remembered love. And she would fondle her memories like gilded jewels, or tender swallows newly-born; and she kept them locked in a box carved of scented amber, and hid it in her breast. And each day she would open it and renew the taste of sweet and bitter love from long ago and drink it deep into the runnels of her white bosom, until they would again dissolve and gall her lonely heart with sadness.

And for many years she clung like this to her jewels of remembrance, and loved not the world.

Then one day it happened that an angel came and knelt before her in a shady cove where she was sleeping. And he laid his head in her lap; and she in her sleep did stroke his auburn curls, which warmed her sullen heart. Then the morning bird-song aroused her from her pleasant slumber and she beheld this gentle stranger, with his warm hair silent in her lap. And she was frightened and could not speak, but stroked his head and called to him. And he awoke and lifted his head, and looked at her with smiling eyes, eyes as blue and wide as the clearest summer sky, and bright and infinite as the million stars of summer night. And she cried out and placed a hand to her heart; but still she continued to look into his eyes. And therein she saw the million bright stars, each one as white and sweet as morning milk; and she saw each star spin and curve into a world of shape and color and sound; and inside each star she beheld one of the many tender jewels that she had kept locked inside her scented chest. She saw the star that held the moment of her lover's first embrace; and the one that held the moment of their secret kiss; and the one where he drank his warm red wine; and the one where he spoke of God and of himself; and the one where she touched his cheek; and the one where she washed his white shirt; and she saw the sunlight on his hair, and the dew under their bare feet, and the sleeping village in the valley below, and a million, million more.

But then, as she looked, she began to see the angel's forehead as well as the jewels; and she looked again, and saw his rosy cheeks as well; and looked again, and saw his smiling mouth as well; and looked again, and saw his head and shoulders too, and then his bronze wings and crimson tunic and leather sandals, and the happy cove with its dashing steams and cypress wands, and the bright blue sky and sun, and the million stars above them. And she saw all of these things at once; and the fire in her heart blazed as white as any of those jewels; and she was happy, and frightened, and lonely, and contented; and she could not speak, but she did sing; and she could not hear, but she did listen; and the angel rose and said these words to her:

"Such is our love that we would yearn for what has been, and hold it to us like a fluttering dove or struggling bear cub. And such is the way of the world, that these tender jewels of light forever dance and tease our yearning eyes, but forever fade away as we would catch and keep them. Yet they are here, where they have always been and always shall remain. And if we see them and collect them and rejoice in their sweet light, as we do rejoice in the million jewels of eventide, so will they always burn for us, and we will burn for them. Now I will string your jewels, which have been locked inside your heart, and make a gleaming necklace, which I will place around your ivory neck. And you will walk and laugh, and pluck many a sweet jewel, and slide it sweetly on your thread; and you will always wear it for the world to see and for you to rejoice in. And you will know that it is always there for you, and that you are here for this."

And he finished with his words and opened his burnished wings; and with his supple fingers he gathered up all those jewels and put them on a string of starry thread. And this he placed around her neck, and kissed her burning forehead; and then like the fire in her heart, he rose into the sky and spread himself in quiet gold across the heavens.

And this young maiden smiled, and was no longer grieved; and she went away into the world and loved everyone she knew; and they did love her in return, and gave her many jewels for her string.

Harps at Midnight

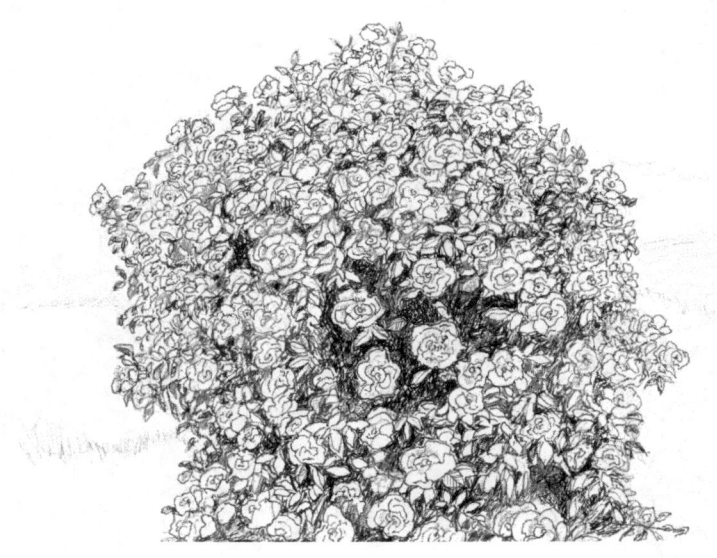

for Nette

Harps at Midnight

THE CUCKOO CLOCK SANG the hour of five. The cat sat on the floor in front of it once again, and its head shook abruptly with every reappearance of the wooden bird. Günter was sitting in the parlor with his large sketch pad on his lap. On the table before him a bronze Orpheus plucked silent enchantment from a lyre resting on its knee. The figure stared slightly upward, as though soon expecting to receive a host of charmed swallows, or even impossible Hermes himself with his long gilded wand. The old artist was nearly stone deaf, and he relished the silence that surrounded him. He watched his hands describe to paper the statue's head and body, and with little strokes he lingered over details of the thumb and fingers that caressed the magic strings. This work made him consider the appropriateness of his subject as it related to his own life, and he found himself reminiscing a little as he drew.

Like the great Beethoven of nearly a hundred years ago, Günter, who also came from Bonn, had felt premonitions of deafness as early on as his twenty-sixth year. This malady fortunately did not inhibit his architectural profession and, after the initial suffering of his increasing quiet had passed, the man actually began to prefer his hushed existence. His visual powers became more and more acute. His ability to render form and line developed into a cunning mastery. At the age of thirty-five he abandoned architecture altogether and devoted himself entirely to drawing and painting. A few years later he moved to Denmark and purchased a comfortable house in Charlottenlund, not far from the Ulov residence where he now lived and served as cook and general housekeeper. He had managed for many years to earn a reasonable living selling landscapes and doing portraits for the wealthy families of Copenhagen. His affliction had enabled him to concentrate his powers of attention on details that easily eluded the average person, and his entire portfolio of work was marked by this singular quality of exhibiting every rose leaf, every eyelash, every blade of grass, every tone of color and shadow that could either be seen or imagined. His wife Maria once fancied that her artist husband saw the world as through an enormous lens, a Van Eyck world in which detail after detail of object and figure stood forth in silent relief like distant, multi-faceted jewels. Günter himself often considered it a privilege to be able to pursue the inward aspirations of his art free from the world's routine clamor. It was as though he moved and lived and worked inside a little chapel nestled deep within the silent forest and prayed alone to his artistic deity for guidance. And what this deity revealed was the clear three-dimensional world before him, which he faithfully rendered to paper and canvas just the way he saw it.

When Maria died, Günter was lonely and unhappy. He had had no illusions that devotion to his art could replace human companionship. He had also begun to regret his and Maria's childless marriage. The offspring that hung in the drawing rooms of Hellerup and in all the shops along the Kompaniestraede could no longer give him the pleasure they had evoked during their gestation, much less delight him with their mature accomplishments or invite him over for the holidays. The artist had lived alone for almost a year, and he was even preparing to sell his home and move back to Germany when Fru Ulov wrote to him. She knew about Günter's circumstances. She was also well aware that his keen attention to detail was reflected equally in his clean household and ample table as it was in his oils and charcoals. The man was delighted to receive three rooms at the top of the large grey house, and the opportunity to busy himself with daily household responsibilities was a welcome compliment to his hours at the easel. Fru Ulov, her sister-in-law, Clara, and her son, Jorgen, were now the only occupants of an at one time very active residence. And to Günter's observation, each of them seemed to carry on an entirely separate existence, like individual objects in one of his own paintings.

His thoughts began to turn around the Ulov family as he worked and reworked the statue's hands and arms. The lyre had become bent recently such that the strings were actually interleaved with the strumming hand. Günter's annoyance at the damage had quickly melted into a fascination with the new impression, and it was just this that had prompted him to put the statue to paper.

He had been aware during these reminiscences of the attentive jerking of the cat's head in the next room, but it was several minutes before the significance of it dawned on him.

"Oh! Nein, nein, nein, nein, nein," he muttered to himself through clenched teeth, something he always did when in a sudden rush. He tossed the pad on the sofa and glanced at his pocket watch. It was indeed well into Fru Jepsen's tea hour. She might have even called down to him a few times in the past fifteen minutes, something that she, in her frequent fits of annoyance, could never refrain from doing. He was in the kitchen in a moment and nimbly set about boiling water, warming milk, and preparing a plate of sandwiches. Many times, in circumstances like this, Günter could not help noticing the incongruity that existed between his internal agitation and the silent objects around him. The pans, bottles, tins, plates, cutlery, everything just sat there dumb and motionless, while he hurried to and fro and grabbed one or another of them. Only the cat perched on the counter edge would occasionally coil its tail or rub its face with a paw. And once again, as he became more and more impatient with the slow boiling kettle and the dull bread knife and the lack of butter, his internal clamor grew louder and still louder and the windows and table and cabinets quieter and still quieter. So now, in his haste, he piled everything together at random onto a large silver tray—spilling some hot water all over the sandwiches in the process—grasped it firmly in his two small hands and tottered down the hallway, with the cat trailing after.

Unfortunately, what Günter had not realized during the previous quarter hour was that there was indeed real chaos occurring in the external world. Ever since the stroke of five, Fru Jepsen had been standing on the second-floor landing shouting down at the artist and stomping her foot with great ferocity. This time the cat had made a real lunge for the wooden bird and in the process had toppled two vases to the floor with a terrific crash. Niels, the postman, had rapped several times, first at the door and then at the window, trying in vain to get Günter's attention. Finally he had tossed two large packages into the hedge and walked away. The dog barked and snarled after him, and then sank its jaws into one of the boxes and began tossing and shaking it about with several growls of animal amusement. And, most unfortunate of all, the poor man was unable to hear, as he approached the staircase near the main foyer with his awkward burden, the sharp smack of the front gate, the hasty footsteps on the pavement and the muffled shouts of "No! No! No!" that grew louder and louder as they neared the front door. The old man placed one foot on the bottom step; the door burst open; the young man, still shouting "No!", flew into the servant and gave him a great shove and then tore up the stairs two at a time. Günter hit the wooden floor full on his back. Porcelain, pots and sandwiches flew everywhere. The hot milk splattered all over the cat. It shrieked and careened down the hallway. Hot tea burned the man's neck and shoulder. The young man's shouts continued all the way up three flights of stairs and were then punctuated by a huge door slam.

Günter was enraged. He rushed up the stairs to the room and marched in without knocking. Jorgen was lying on the bed with a pillow pulled tightly over his head. When the artist came in and began shouting inarticulate curses at him in German, the young man threw the pillow in his face and shouted back at him in fully-articulate Danish. Fru Jepsen came to the doorway and chimed in her own unhappy epithets. But the young man soon became more aggressive, and he pushed both older people out of the room with a second great slam of the door. He then dragged the bed in front of it and sat down on the floor, pulling the pillow tight around his ears once again.

Both the servant and the woman were terribly shaken. Clara went up to her room and sat in a chair and stared straight ahead of her without drying her face. Günter gathered up the mess in the foyer and returned to the kitchen to prepare tea once again. The cupboards and counters were still immobile and unresponsive. The cat sat on the floor and licked itself contentedly. Günter piled all the broken porcelain on a piece of cardboard. He stood at the sink and dabbed his neck with a cold wet towel. For a moment, he regretted the silence that surrounded him.

Fru Clara Jepsen could not have been expected to give any coherent news to Fru Ulov, not even about something as outrageous as Jorgen's behavior that afternoon. Not that there was any real antagonism between her and her late brother's wife. Clara had from her earliest years been remarkably adept at telling stories. As a child she had often charmed her two younger sisters to sleep with elaborate tales about witches and Nordic heroes.

In later years her fame as a schoolteacher was due largely to her ability to interweave instruction in simple arithmetic, geography, and history with fables about the multiplying Giant or the good fairy with the magic memory for names and dates. And most of all she enjoyed keeping her little Clara wide-eyed every evening until the child dropped off into her own story world. But this little girl contracted pneumonia the winter of her eleventh year and did not survive into the following spring. The woman kept her grief to herself for a long time, and she seemed more and more to assuage her sorrow with an ever-increasing interest in her fantastic method of instruction. Then one afternoon she began telling her class about a poor little girl who did not dress properly for the cold and the terrible consequences of such neglect. And then she burst into tears. A few days later Fru Jepsen was gently offered an early retirement, and she and her husband moved to a small farm in Jutland. The woman had attempted for a long time to write down a series of her best stories; indeed, the old schoolmaster had arranged for their publication well in advance. Yet Clara's works were never again free from the stains of lament, and even self-judgment. To state it another way, she could never take the reality out of her fantasy. Everything that she experienced around her, and all her past memories, became one elaborate fairy tale with an unhappy ending. No immediate circumstance, no fresh impression of sound or light, no new acquaintance, nor journey to another portion of the Danish countryside, nothing could penetrate her world without it becoming another chapter in her pensive wonderland. It was not long after her husband died that she joined the Ulov household, and it was not long before Fru Ulov learned to ignore her sister-in-law's anecdotes with polite assurances that everything would be well and that she would personally ward off any ogre or troll that attempted to usurp their happy home. There were many moments, especially in recent months, when the woman seemed to be regaining a certain degree of serenity and composure. But no voice ever whispered so fondly in Clara's ear as did her own. It still told her everything, and it continued to transform the world before her eyes into another turn of the fairybook's page.

Günter knew all of this and so had an equal disregard for Fru Jepsen's reliability. That evening he sat with Jette Ulov on the sofa and wrote out an elaborate account in both words and pictures, as was his custom, of Jorgen's growing irascibility and its culmination in the episode of this afternoon. Fru Ulov, as was her custom, made no real attempt to understand what the artist told her, although she believed everything he said, but decided instead to call upon her long-time friend and the community's local minister, Torben Nielsen, to spend an hour or so with her son the next evening. This the good man was quite willing to do, and to everyone's surprise Jorgen gave no resistance. Günter prepared a delightful meal for the household and their guest, and afterward the ladies went into the parlor with their knitting while the minister followed Jorgen upstairs to his room with a bottle of wine. Herr Nielsen considered some years later that it was probably for the best that he alone had heard the young man's story. Certainly it would have availed nothing to offer an explanation to the artist-servant or the ladies. And the change that it brought about in his own life was so thorough, and at the same time so unassuming, that he would have inevitably been labeled by the public as an unhappy counterpart to Clara's despair.

Jorgen opened the window and sat by it with his elbow propped up on the sill. He refused the minister's offer of a glass of wine and stared out into the quiet evening sky for many moments. Then he began speaking. Throughout most of his story, he continued staring out the window and only occasionally turned toward his listener, who sat quietly and sipped away at the bottle.

"You know, Herr Minister, it is commonly agreed that either things exist in the world as they are or that we project or imagine things to be other than they are. It is also commonly agreed that in many cases we cannot know for certain what is real and what imaginary. What is perhaps often taken to be the yardstick of reality is the degree to which we can actually see, feel, taste and touch the particular object or phenomenon in question. But, of course, it is not impossible for our senses to deceive us. So that, even when we plainly see or hear something with all our normal clarity, it is quite likely that our own or someone else's mind can reject any perception that seems to defy common sense." He gave a short laugh and then cleared his throat. "Please do not get the impression now that I am going to present a philosophical lecture tonight. I am sure you are far more familiar with all these theories than I. But I think what I just said helps in some way to explain the misery I am now in.

"Up until last month I was living with Junilde Ericksen. You know her family? We were renting a little house up north very close to the sea. There are a few other cottages in the neighboring wood, but there is enough distance between them all to give each household plenty of privacy. In fact, for the first five months we lived there, Junilde and I saw only two other people in the area. But in the evenings you could see smoke coming from every chimney.

"About two months ago we were sitting up in bed one evening and gazing at the stars through an open window. Junilde knows a lot about the various constellations and galaxies, and she was describing some of them to me. I can, for instance, easily make out the Pleiades over there. Anyway, as we talked and made a few jokes about seeing the future in the stars, I suddenly became aware of the gentle sound of someone playing a harp. The experience of it was such that I had not heard the sound begin, but gradually noticed that it was there while we conversed. It was a very pleasant sound, as the sound of a harp usually is, and for many minutes I simply enjoyed it and listened to Junilde at the same time. Whoever was playing the instrument stopped and started many times, and at one point I said, 'How pleasant it is listening to someone practice on the harp. Even when they get it wrong, it sounds pretty.' I said nothing more about it that evening, and Junilde only gave me a strange laugh at those words of mine.

"The next two days I was at home alone. I needed to work on my dissertation, so Junilde went to Rosskilde to stay with her mother. The first afternoon I wrote and studied well into the night without any food or drink. When the clock struck ten—or maybe it was eleven—I paused for some bread and cheese, and drank some snaps, and then went back to my books. But as I sat there absorbed in reading and taking notes, I heard the gentle music again. Like the previous evening, I did not hear it actually begin but gradually noticed that it was there. It was so light, so fragile. The heaviness of my mind and body seemed like iron by comparison. I put down my pen and moved my chair over to the window. Two other cottages were visible through the trees. Both had lights glimmering in their windows and smoke curling quietly above them. I gazed at one house and then the other for a long time to see which contained the harpist. It was difficult to do this because many times, as I strained my eyes and ears, the music would go away—and then return when I thought it was over. I sat there for almost an hour. Finally the music stopped. I had not noticed it stop. I also did not notice the lights go out in the other cottages either. It just became black."

With his last few words Jorgen had become more and more sad, and at the close of his story he simply stared in silent vacancy. Herr Nielsen felt obliged to say something, but before he could speak the young man turned to him. "This is all childish, isn't it? This is all nonsense? But you don't understand. The next night it was the same. And the night after that, and the night after that. And now, now it is all day! Every day! Everywhere!" He rose to his feet and shouted "Everywhere!" again. Herr Nielsen stood up as well. He did this out of imitation more than anything else. The good minister was used to listening to people's problems over a few glasses of wine. But such unrestraint, such unpredictability was new to him. He began to consider what he should say, or whether he should even restrain the youth. But while he was thinking this over, Jorgen gave a long sigh and sat back down again. The minister did the same, and poured himself another glass. "Are you sure you wouldn't like some? It might help."

Jorgen was looking at the Pleiades again. "There is no harp, Herr Nielsen. There is no harp. No one hears the music. No one. The evening Junilde returned I asked her if she found it pleasant. She giggled at me. 'Find what pleasant?' 'The harp', I said, 'he's practicing now.' 'Who?' 'I don't know who, but we hear the music don't we?' 'What music?' 'Junilde, please, you hear it? Listen! You hear it now?' She gave me such a blank look. I never thought I was capable of such anger, not with her. I thought she was teasing me. The next day I visited the two cottages. In one lives a carpenter and his wife with four small boys. 'What is... harp?' the man asked me. In the other lives an elderly couple, both long retired. The woman was very polite in denying ever seeing or hearing such an instrument around these parts, although her daughter had a friend who played one in the school orchestra some years ago. You know, Her Nielsen, I believed her, I really did. But I was becoming desperate. I could not conceive that such rage, such violence could possess me. I pushed the old woman aside and turned over all her furniture, boxes, and chests in vain. I broke a water pitcher in the process, and handed her a fifty-kroner note as I walked out of the house. Junilde heard about it from the old man a few days later, and then her earful became mine. But by then I didn't care. I was crazed. I could hear it everywhere. The first time I heard it in daylight was at the large open market. I had just purchased Junilde some beautiful gold earrings to try and make up for my behavior. As the woman was wrapping them up and I handed her the money, it was there again. Like always. There before I knew it was there. I looked at the woman and she smiled back at me, and I thought, 'Now, now they hear!' I told her what a beautiful sound it made. She laughed and said yes, the coins were dropping into her box today like silver bells. 'No', I said, 'no, the harp! The harp!' even though by then I knew it was no use. And there were moments then—even while I shouted, even when I got in a scuffle with the man standing next to me— when the music still continued, a gentle whisper in my head.

"I tell you, Herr Minister, it is maddening, maddening. You know everything else, I'm sure. Junilde and I just couldn't stay together. It's all my fault, of course. I moved here, she went back to Rosskilde, and I am almost a lunatic. I cannot work. I will surely miss the deadline for my exam and my paper and I don't care. What I do care about is my destructiveness. Everyone always thought I was so gentle, just like a harp itself. I thought the same. But I am murderous. I fight with people. I shout at them. I break things. I was sitting in the parlor a few days ago when the music came, and I tried to wrench the lyre out of that statue's hand. And yesterday, for the first time, what happened? I went for a walk in the park, I sat under a tree with Shakespeare's sonnets, and then, from across the field, or up in the tree, or

God knows where, there came the sound of not one, but two, two harps! The music was warm and golden. I actually let myself go for a few moments and enjoyed it to the full. The sounds became richer and stronger, and I soon felt that an angelic ecstasy would carry me away. But as I sat there and listened, a group of people walked by chattering among themselves and tossing sticks for their dogs. They heard nothing. One girl looked at me and smiled. And there I was, sitting under a tree and listening to these harps. Surely I was going insane. I ran off home and shouted to myself as loudly as I could to drown out the sound. Two of the dogs chased me for a while and nipped at my ankles. So when I entered the house, you can understand my rage." He paused. "Or maybe you can't. Oh, of course, why should you? Why should you?"

Herr Nielsen watched the young man's shoulders rise and fall with unsteady breath. But he watched this for only the briefest moment and then began speaking. He explained to Jorgen that such experiences were not so uncommon and that they were surely not a sign of madness. He said it was important to consider the stability of his present circumstances. He should, for one thing, marry Junilde Ericksen. This was the surest way for both of them to overcome any personal difficulties they were bound to encounter. Here he laughed and admitted that he had reached a similar impasse just before his final examination, but that in his case it was a fondness for the bottle that had stood in his way. Yet he went through it all, and was now a successful preacher and theologian, and the happy father of three children. And he still enjoyed his wine. All of this was said to the youth in his usual easy manner. Jorgen had grown completely still and silent during his remarks, but Herr Nielsen was aware that perhaps not everything he said was received in full. He was not aware, however, that the reason for this was the still unwelcome distraction of another, more ephemeral voice.

Herr Nielsen stopped speaking and saw Jorgen look at him. Both were silent for a moment. "I remember as well..." the minister began again. "Please, sir," Jorgen said quietly. "I thank you for your time, and for listening to my silly complaints. But I am exhausted. And yes, you are right. I should finish the paper, and then go to Paris for a month as I planned to." The minister rose and pressed his hand warmly, "Good night, then, my friend." The house was silent as Herr Nielsen went downstairs, so he simply took his coat and departed.

The night was unusually still. Herr Nielsen did not meet anyone. He also did not hear anything. No voices, no footfall, no horse hoofs, no wind. The trees were black and motionless. Paper and leaves littered the gutters, but nothing stirred. The stars were quiet jewels, the houses and shops muted and dark. He only heard his own footsteps and brisk respiring. So as he walked, he began to think more about Jorgen's story, and soon his thoughts filled up the stillness around him with a loud and successful clamor.

Torben Kristoff Nielsen was an intelligent man. His intelligence was of the kind that made light of most theorems, formulas, philosophical outlooks, forms of expression and religious dogma. He did not make light of them, though, in the sense of considering it all insignificant. Rather was it the case that Herr Nielsen readily understood and digested every idea that came his way. He liked ideas, in every field of knowledge, and above all he liked his ability to comprehend them. Early on in his university studies he experienced the revelation of how to understand what he read and heard about. He saw that every idea, every system, was based upon one or another simple truth, one or another moment of insight when a new chink in the wall let in an additional ray of light for someone to catch it up. So by grasping these simple truths, by getting to the source of whatever Hegel or Voltaire or Aristotle was trying to say, Torben was able to comprehend and elaborate upon their work without paying attention to all the details. In this way he had surpassed all his schoolmates both in essential knowledge and in freedom of analysis. And in this way he had still enjoyed his time at the taverns well into the midnight hours.

There is no question but that new light stings the eyes when the darkness is pierced. Torben read and studied the stinging experiences of others, but such revelations were not for him. There was no need. He accumulated and comprehended the experiences of all the noble witnesses of the past. What they had to say, what they had constructed, was sufficient enough light for humanity to continue unimpeded for many years to come. And it was certainly enough for Herr Nielsen. Even now as he walked home, he was reconsidering his new essay on St. John's

Revelations in view of the things Jorgen had told him. There were, he thought, some interesting connections there.

At one point he looked up and beheld the majesty of the stars in the clear evening sky. He knew about the stars too. Probably better than Junilde did. He stopped and studied them for a while, and as he did so he considered again how unusually quiet the town was. Perhaps there had been an accident? Or a fire? Or even another big party at the Mannheims? But no, he would have been invited. There was nothing to do now, no one to talk to, and, try as he could, Torben heard not a sound.

Silence always made Torben uncomfortable. He was a great talker, and people enjoyed him equally as well by the fireside and in the tavern as in the pulpit on Sunday. He always had friendly words or clever anecdotes or accurate observations for everyone he encountered. He always found a way to begin a conversation, and all his friends and acquaintances always found a way either to listen appreciatively or to excuse themselves when their limit was reached. It was true, Torben tended to miss certain nuances of feeling that often passed between people. Those little pauses in conversation when no one could find a word to say, the briefest moments of frank eye contact, the sudden awareness of the sound of his own voice and the wish not to hear it; these almost imperceptible silences yawned open unfamiliar abysses all around him, and the wheels of his tongue and intellect were always called upon to close them up again. Yet for the longest time he never felt he was avoiding something. These experiences were unnecessary. People wanted him the way he was. Even on quiet evenings at home, when his wife sat and looked at him, and he at her, he seldom went further than to ask himself what he was not doing that needed accomplishment.

A few clouds began to pass in front of the Pleiades. Torben gazed far down the street. Away in the distance he thought he saw a horse and carriage cross over, and he waited for the accompanying rattle and driver's call. There were none. A light draft of air caressed his face. He watched some low-hanging branches bob up and down in the gentle breeze. They looked like the strumming fingers of a merry troubadour. The silence remained.

The following afternoon Jorgen Ulov threw a chair through one of the dining room windows. Günter shouted more incoherent abuse than ever, and when Jorgen crouched down and put his hands over his ears, the old man thought he was ridiculing him and almost wept with anger. A message was sent to Fru Ulov at the State Museum, and she came home at once almost in tears herself. She went into the parlor with Jorgen and had Günter pull out and lock the big sliding doors. Mother and son then carried on the following conversation in complete privacy, although it only occurred to Fru Ulov a few days later that Clara and Günter were rather unlikely eavesdroppers.

"Jorgen, my dear, what is it? Why are you doing these things?" "I hear the harps and I cannot stand it." "Well, pretend they're not there." "But I'm probably pretending they are there." "Then stop pretending." "I can't." "Why don't you and Junilde get married?" "She thinks I'm not interested anymore.

Maybe she's right." "Is she right?" "No." "Well?" "She doesn't hear them." "What?" "The harps." "What harps?" "Mother, these crazy sounds. I hear them everywhere. But no one else does." "Must you break windows because no one else hears what you hear?" "It helps a little." "Maybe you should practice the harp yourself." "I'd probably ruin that, too." "Jorgen, this has to stop. Didn't Herr Nielsen give you any advice?" "Who knows?" "He's a very intelligent man." "Everybody has their excuse." "What do you... for what?" "Mother, I am sorry. I wish things were different." "Well, listen. It is your birthday next Saturday, and I want to have a nice dinner for you. I've already invited Birte—unfortunately Jens cannot make it—and I want Junilde there as well. And I was even thinking of Herr and Fru Nielsen. Isn't that splendid?" "So you actually think Günter will cook for me?" "Of course! He adores you. Just, please, don't go near his paintings." "Don't worry." "Is that over then?" "Something's over, I suppose."

Fru Ulov was completely relieved by these last words, although why she was relieved she did not at all consider. There were many things that passed through the mind and heart of this good woman that she did not long reflect upon. Over the years she had come to believe that the gentle touch in all things at all times produced the best results, at least for herself. She often recalled how as a young girl she used to play by the pond and watch dragonflies scud across the surface, leaving behind the most ephemeral tremble of ripples. And similar impressions, like wisps of dusty snow and the intricate web of lace napkins, collected inside of her and formed an equally fine gauze for filtering through the momentums of everyday life. Almost everything went through her. The feelings and situations that did linger in her memory were, by their very proximity, recognized as part of her real world, and all other new or unusual events that she encountered were either gathered into this world or allowed to pass on and disappear like those tiny waves. Because of this, Fru Ulov loved her family, loved her household, loved art and noticed little else. Most people who knew her envied her her serenity and single-minded devotion to family and career. The few people who knew her well did not envy, but at the same time could little comprehend, her unusual light-heartedness and detachment.

Both Jorgen and his sister, Birte, grew up under this influence, or lack of influence, and both early acquired the ability to say and do whatever they felt like without much fear of opposition. They were, most fortunately, not aggressive children, and in many ways their natures were rather similar to their mother's. Still, Jorgen especially could seldom resist the urge to smash down Birte's snowman or take apart the clocks that his father kept and tinkered with in his little workshop. But the boy was also fascinated by books, especially poetry, and his parents were eventually quite relieved to find their son channeling his energies into schoolwork rather than their picket fence. It was not long before he was channeling his energies into something else as well, and eventually Jorgen was making friends with another girl in the neighborhood almost every month. His mother and father felt with some amount of pride that it would not be many years before the family would see the beginning of a new generation of Ulovs occupying the same house and grounds and continuing as a significant force in Danish society. Even after her husband's sudden passing, Fru Ulov never relinquished this picture of her son's and her family's future. So despite Jorgen's increasing dissatisfaction with himself and his obvious unwillingness to prepare the way for a "normal" existence, and despite the Ulov household no longer being the center for social gatherings and artistic tete-a-tetes that it once was, and despite the movement toward individual interests and away from a sense of clannish fidelity that everyone in the immediate family was experiencing, Jette Ulov continued to let all present circumstances pass through her innermost heart and nurtured only the triumphant repose that was promised her so long ago.

Jorgen himself was aware of his mother's longings, but only occasionally did his destructive impulse wish to startle her into a glimpse at his own world, a world that recognized how seldom things were what they seemed to be. His mother was never unhappy. Junilde pointed this out to him many times. And, she continued one evening, who is to say that what is most real is what you least suspect? Was not the most real thing that which affected you most deeply? Maybe people's dreams always come true. Jorgen said nothing to all this, mostly because it kept both Junilde and his mother happy. But the young man could not escape moments of sarcasm when he considered that no one ever arrives at your doorstep with your salvation in their pockets. He often tended to curse, rather than to bless, coincidence and aspiration. He had a gift for seeing through appearances, and his frank behavior with people won him equally as many enemies as friends. But Jorgen did not wish otherwise. To be popular was to be insincere. When something is not pleasant, when something is not honest or beautiful or skillful, why call it so? Like many sensitive people his age, it was difficult for him not to see truth as something tinged with the ordinary. When the mystery disappears, we are still left with dirty underwear and no credit at the bank. In this way the gentle sounds that haunted him remained something to fight with and became the mystery that found its explanation in the failings of his own life.

The morning of his twenty-fourth birthday Jorgen found a scroll of paper tied up with a red ribbon outside the door of his room. When he untied it and spread it open on his desk, he was at the first instant surprised into stillness not unlike the statue he saw there represented. Many feelings passed through him in quick succession, but most of all he was touched by Günter's gesture and felt obliged to be as kind as possible to the man from then on. He turned the picture over and placed several books on top of it.

Jorgen went into Copenhagen in the early afternoon to meet Junilde at the station. Birte had arrived soon after he left to help Jette and Clara clean the house and prepare the table. As always with large affairs like this one, Günter kept the kitchen entirely to himself and set out tea and sandwiches for the ladies in the conservatory.

It was a warm spring day, summer was approaching, and the welcome sunlight brought more and more people out into their gardens and along the avenues. Birte enjoyed watching other people promenade or stand in groups under the chestnut trees, and she sat by the parlor window after lunch for almost an hour. She was already feeling a little tipsy from some chilled German wine, so when she saw Junilde and her brother walking toward the house hand in hand, she was rather vociferous in announcing it to the rest of the household.

"Mama! Mama! Everything is just perfect now!"

The evening was indeed a near perfect event. Torben Nielsen first offered a champagne toast to the memory of Jorgen Sr. and then gave a brief speech—brief for him—about the happy future of that man's son and his bride-to-be, and finished with a recapitulation of what Jette Ulov had single-handedly accomplished over the years by encouraging young Danish artists and promoting their works to the general public. Jorgen himself followed these words with expressions of gratitude to family and friends and the hope that he would someday be worthy of their generosity toward him, a generosity which of late he seemed entirely undeserving. Everyone scoffed at this final statement, except Junilde and Günter, and Torben refilled everyone's glass and proceeded into a series of anecdotes about the early years of his and Marte's marriage and the difficulties of finding the right kind of house and the right kind of horses. These stories continued from the conservatory, where they had had their hors d'oeuvres, through into the dining room, where the first plates of fish and salad were passed around. At one point Jette mentioned that one of her favorite works of Günter's was a series of sketches of rare horses, and then she quickly asked Marte if she was familiar with them. Marte said yes, they almost bought one, and Torben began to follow that with a loud explanation of why they did not, even though his mouth was full of herring, but Jorgen came in first with a proud description of the artist's birthday gift to him. The conversation continued with various pleasantries and gentle waves of laughter while more and more dishes of meat and vegetables and fresh bread kept arriving from the kitchen. Torben continued refilling all the glasses right from where he was sitting simply by extending his arm and the bottle across the table. Birte and Junilde sat next to each other and constantly suppressed giggles between them over Herr Nielsen's procedure. Birte had drunk far too much, and Junilde hardly ever had more than a glass of sherry at any one meal, so both girls were blushing and dreamy-eyed as the evening wore on.

At one point Marte began describing the difficulties of getting her little Olga to say a prayer of thank you to God and the angels before going to bed each evening. She told how the girl once screamed and thrashed her legs in the air and said that she didn't know any God or angels and only wanted to dream about her white horses and candy-cane friends. Torben became a little embarrassed at this and said, "It takes a certain degree of maturity to have converse with the Lord. We cannot expect formal worship from someone so innocent."

Jorgen laughed at this statement and remarked, "So you need to be a sinner in order to pray properly."

"I cannot say, Jorgen, I haven't studied the subject deeply enough as yet. But from what I have read so far there seem to be indications that a certain degree of recognition of one's own baseness is a necessary prerequisite to intercourse with They who stand above us. There is a pamphlet I recently came across at the library about this. I could show..."

"Well, if you've never done anything wrong," Junilde said, "and if you're always happy and kind, then where is the baseness? You're almost saying that good people can't go to heaven."

"Why should they?" Jorgen said to her. Junilde stared at him for a moment and then lowered her eyes. She said nothing else while at the table.

"No, but this notion of good and bad doesn't work," Torben went on. "We need a different basis for moral principles. Everything depends upon action and inaction. There was a recent essay by that Englishman—what was his name, Jorgen?

"Hadley."

"I agree with Marte," Jette Ulov said. "Children need to know about the Divine, even if they struggle against the idea for years and years. After all, before they are born, they are kicking about inside of us. I'd feel more comfortable knowing that they were fighting than if they simply ignored the matter altogether."

"But most people do ignore it," Birte said.

Jette Ulov took a sip of her wine and did not continue. Up to this point in the dinner neither Clara nor Günter had contributed to the conversation. Günter was not shy in company. He kept a notepad with him at all times, and this evening he was watching everyone's lips most carefully. Just after Birte's comment, he began writing something on his pad while Torben began explaining the substance of this Mr. Hadley's essay.

Clara also seemed to be enjoying herself this evening. Her face was calm, though a little distant, and she had been most polite in passing around the plates and seeing that everyone had had enough to eat. She ate and drank little herself. At this moment when the minister began philosophizing, she became a trifle more withdrawn and leaned back in her chair with folded arms. She watched Torben place both his hands on the table and repeatedly raise one and then the other of them and say, "Action. Inaction. Action. Inaction…" And then she sighed, cleared her throat, and began speaking. Her voice was gentle and even, and she spoke right through Herr Nielsen's discourse. Everyone at the table had the same experience of gradually becoming aware of Clara and her story and of gradually hearing the minister's voice recede into a mutter and finally disappear:

"Many years ago there lived on the island of Fjune a happy couple by name of Hans and Hildur. Hans was a tailor, and a happy one at that, and he mended holes and loose buttons as carefully and joyfully as he made costumes and uniforms and waistcoats. Hildur kept a happy cottage, with flower boxes in every window and shiny copper pots hanging in the kitchen, and she shook the carpets and dusted the door jambs as carefully and joyfully as she baked her bread and biscuits and apple tarts. Now the real secret of all their happiness was their little girl, Annie, a girl who wore long yellow pigtails and liked to chase after the crows and magpies in the fields. 'Why do they run away?' she would ask Hildur with tears in her eyes. 'I only want to stroke their wings.' On Annie's sixth birthday, Hans came home with a large brown sack in his arms that had a long pink ribbon trailing out of it and fluttering in the wind. He took his little girl by the hand and led her into the garden and dug a hole deep into the moist brown earth. Then he took something long and scaly out of the bag and said to his daughter, 'Here is a present for you, my child, to celebrate your sixth year on this earth. And if you watch your new friend very carefully, he will soon have something quite wonderful to say to you.' And saying this Hans placed the bottom of the stumpy little figure into the hole and filled some loose dirt around it. Annie was wide-eyed at the thought of a new toy, but her happiness quickly changed to bewilderment at the sight of this strange little stick man with three twisted arms and little prickly pointer things all over his body. That first afternoon she came running into the house crying and showed her mother her little round palm all covered with blood. 'I tried to pet him and he bit me,' she said, and big tears rolled down her face. Hildur knelt down in front of her daughter and said, 'Well, your friend doesn't always need to be touched like this, but if you keep watching him every day, he will soon speak such very nice things.' So Annie withheld her tears and wiped her face, and every day she came and said hello to the little man and waited to see what wonderful things he would tell her. As the days went by and the sun would shine more warmly and the bees would linger about the new petals, the little man did indeed begin to do something. First Annie noticed little red whiskers on the tips of his fingers and the top of his head. Then one morning she saw them change into little tight lips the color of the ribbon that was still tied around his neck. And each day Annie became more and more excited as the lips became bigger and fuller and more plentiful, so that at any moment they seemed ready to shout their message in the child's ears. Annie would stand in front of her friend for a long, long time and wait for him to speak. One day she thought that perhaps he did not speak so loudly after all, but whispered like grandfather Poul, so she brought her face right up to one of the pink mouths with its dozens of lips—and he gave her a kiss! So sweet and fragrant, sweeter than anything she had ever felt before. She shrieked with delight and jumped back laughing, and then slowly came forward once more and put her face near another one of his mouths. And then another kiss! And more, and more! And so every morning before she went to school and every afternoon when she came home again, Annie would say hello and kiss her little friend, and pour a cup of water at his feet, for Hildur told Annie how much he liked that. All of this kissing and attraction seemed to make him very happy indeed, because his kisses became sweeter and his lips became fuller and more plentiful than ever. One morning when Annie came out to say hello, she was surprised to find some of her friend's lips open all the way. 'Oh, Mama!' she called to Hildur. 'Did you hear him say anything? What did he say?' But Hilder said she had not heard and that maybe if Annie went up to him very

close and was very, very quiet, maybe she would catch his words.
And this the child did, and pressed her ear ever so gently next
to his open mouth. She waited for a long time, but soon she had
to run off to school. All day the only thing she could think about
was what her little friend was trying to tell her; and when the
afternoon bell sounded, she ran all the way back home, dropping
her books on the ground several times along the way. She was almost out of breath when she pushed open the front gate, and she
burst through the front door and nearly tripped up her mother,
who was just walking by with a basket of laundry. She threw her
books on the table and ran out into the garden, and then, Oh!
What did she see? Hildur heard Annie crying and hurried out to
her. 'My friend is dead!' She cried. 'He's dead! Why? Why?' She
cried long and loudly and Hilbur sat on the steps and held her
quietly while the girl shook her tender sobs into her mother's bosom. Later Hildur showed the child all her little friend's lips and
told her that no, she didn't ever hear what he finally said, but that
he was only just sleeping now and that soon he would come back
with more kisses than she could possibly receive. And so Annie
kept watching and, sure enough, the red whiskers returned, and
then the tightly puckered lips, and finally the beautiful kisses and
velvet smiles. Again the child listened ever so carefully, but again
she could never quite catch what her little friend was saying.
When he went to sleep for the winter, she often dreamed about
him and about the many places they would visit together once
he learned how to walk; and when he woke up again each summer and started beckoning to her from behind his little hedge

home, she was always there each day to moisten his feet and give him some kind words. This happy friendship lasted for a number of seasons, and Annie learned to accept the funny man's way of curling back his lips and then going to sleep for a long time. Hildur and Hans noticed that a certain understanding seemed to exist between the two friends that they could not share and that indeed Annie told the little man things that no one else could hear. One very hot evening the child went to bed with the window wide open and listened to the leaves whisper secrets to the mild evening air. But after she fell asleep, this whisper grew into a shrewd whistle and then it became very cold and wet and the winds came in and swirled all around the little girl. She awoke next morning hot and shivering, and Hildur kept her covered up in bed and gave her oranges and tea. For several days she stayed hot and sweating, but she never complained and only asked if her little friend was safe, because it had been so very cold the other evening. Hildur assured her that he was fine and that he probably could not wait to see her again and give her a big kiss. One morning she came into Annie's room with a tray of biscuits and a bowl filled with some of the man's tender lips. Annie was sitting up in bed. She was white and cold. Her cheeks were like ivory and her lips were blue, and her eyes were only half open. Hildur sat on the bed and clutched her little chilly hand and called to her many times. The child still breathed, but did not answer. Hildur put her ear right up to the child's lips. Then she began to cry. Big tears rolled down her face. Annie stirred and opened her eyes and smiled at her, 'Oh, Mama,' she said, 'now I know what my little friend is saying.' And she closed her eyes and did not open them ever again."

Neither Jorgen nor Torben heard the end of the story. Once the minister had stopped his explanations, everyone put down their knives and forks and gave Clara their full attention. Torben cleared his throat a few times, and once or twice even began to comment on the woman's narrative. But since no one gave him even the slightest look, he did not continue. And Jorgen was also distracted. He had been so content during most of the meal, and the experience of witnessing Clara speak as she did fascinated him as much as it embarrassed his mother. But before long he was staring in such a way that showed he was not hearing the woman's words. At one point he clutched the table with both hands and gripped it until his knuckles were white. Then he leaned forward on his elbows, partially covering his ears with his hands. He scratched his head. He coughed and turned full around in his chair to face Fru Jepsen. Nothing seemed to help. When Clara began to speak about the cold winds coming into Annie's bedroom, Jorgen sprang out of his chair, sending it skidding back against the wall, and rushed out into the conservatory and from there out into the garden. Junilde leaned forward and watched him go but did not follow. Torben felt both a sense of duty toward mollifying the young man's suffering and a sense of relief at having an excuse for leaving the table. He hurried after him.

It was a warm night. There was a sweet smell of new mown grass and on the other side of the field a group of people could be heard laughing and singing. The sky was clear and full of stars. Torben saw the black shape of Jorgen leaning against the wooden fence behind the hedge at the far side of the garden. He approached the young man quietly and placed a hand on his shoulder. Jorgen did not stir. After a few moments Torben felt a little self-conscious about standing there in the dark touching someone, and so he started to say, "The sensitivity of a woman is difficult…"

Jorgen turned around abruptly and grabbed the minister by his jacket. "Hear them! Please! Please! Try to hear them."

Torben sighed. "Music is surely holy language…"

"No! No! Herr Minister, stop! Listen, please!"

They stood and faced one another. Each man's features were just barely discernible by the other in the darkness. They were quiet for several minutes. The laughter in the distance had stopped. There came the solemn toll of a church bell far away. It rang twelve times. It was quiet again. Torben breathed deeply. He began to perspire. He wiped his brow with his forearm and looked at Jorgen. The young man continued staring at him. Herr Nielsen turned and looked out over the dark field. He glanced up at the stars.

Then he clutched Jorgen's shoulder once again.

"Yes. Yes." First he whispered, and gradually his voice rose to an even tone, "Yes, I hear them now. It… it is a miracle. It is unbelievable. But they are there. They…"

He faced the young man again and took both his shoulders in his hands. "They are there. I don't know how. But…"

Herr Nielsen could not go on, and Jorgen was long past wishing to say anything. They looked at one another, and quiet little tinkles hovered above them.

'Little strands of halo hair/linger on the honey air./Golden children sweet and fair/whisper music everywhere.'

At one point Torben heard Jorgen mutter, "Oh, Herr Nielsen, Herr Nielsen. We can never return. We can never, never…" The two men stood by the fence in the darkness for almost a quarter hour more. Neither of them spoke. When they turned and walked back toward the house, they happened to glance at each other at the same moment. They both laughed.

By now they had somehow expected that the evening was over and that dessert and coffee had lulled everyone into armchairs. So both men were rather surprised to hear, as they entered the conservatory, the muffled shouts and screams and groans of nearly everyone in the household, and they were even more surprised, when they entered the dining room, to find displayed before them the most unexpected chaos and absolute mess that the Ulov residence had probably ever experienced.

Two chairs were knocked over. There were splashes of wine and gravy on the carpet, and over by the window they saw a ragged trail of blood leading into the front room. Another trail of blood led that way from the kitchen; Jorgen pushed open the kitchen door. One of the cupboard doors lay on the floor cracked in several places. Almost all the dishes were also on the floor in a smashed heap, with both the cat and dog busy picking out the remains. But this mess did not nearly startle the men as much as the incongruous cacophony of voices coming from everywhere. Junilde could be heard screaming in the parlor. Günter was also moaning sonorously, although seemingly repressing the urge to express his pain. Above these two unhappy refrains, Clara's voice, as serene and composed as when she had told her story, was repeating reassuring phrases to them both. They could also hear the sound of cloth being dipped in water. And, most remarkable of all, from the first floor landing came the sounds of Jette Ulov shouting at, and even once or twice striking, the usually insolent Birte, who only sobbed and pleaded with her mother to stop.

Torben and Jorgen looked at each other. Clara brushed past them and went into the kitchen for some clean towels. She came out again and glanced over her shoulder as she walked by. "Come on now, gentlemen. No time for philosophy."

She went back into the parlor. Jorgen followed her and sat by Junilde for a few minutes. She was stretched out on the couch, her bloody and bandaged foot dangling over a pot of red water. Günter was sitting in a chair holding his side, which bled all down his thigh and calf. Clara kept pushing away his hands and wiping the wound with a towel. Jorgen kissed Junilde, gave Günter a friendly pat on the shoulder, and went upstairs. Torben stood at the door to the hallway and watched Marte help Fru Jepsen. After a while he walked into the hall with his hands in his pockets. He heard both Jette and Birte sobbing and giving each other apologies, while Jorgen spoke to them about how wonderful the evening had been. Torben sighed and scratched his head. He turned around once more and looked into the parlor.

He shrugged his shoulders, went into the kitchen, and started to work on the pots and pans.

The next day both men were told what had happened. Birte was trying hard not to laugh at Fru Jepsen during the story. When Clara had finished and the lightness of everyone's attention had sounded together like one clear bell, Birte became very red in the face and exploded with laughter into her plate. "What a naughty mother, to leave the window open," she said. This startled everyone at the table, but what followed shook them even more. "Birte!" Jette screamed. She jumped out of her chair, knocking it to the floor, and made right for her daughter. Birte sprang up, knocking her chair over as well, just in time to receive a round slap in the face. The women started shouting at each other, but the delicate Frau Ulov, the serene and composed Fru Ulov, soon silenced her daughter into tears. The others politely began to clear the table. Then Junilde, who had the habit of walking about barefooted, stepped into a large sliver of glass that had been overlooked when the window was replaced. She shrieked and stumbled to her knee. Marte and Clara helped her into the next room, and when Clara began to pull the glass out, Junilde screamed even more with abandon. Fru Jepsen caught up the blood in her own skirt until Marte came back with some towels.

Günter had continued clearing the table. He felt a few pangs of resentment about doing this, but with all the ladies carrying on as they were, he was only too glad to seek refuge in his quiet little chapel. However, the usually obedient objects around him also seemed to be in rebellion tonight. Twice as he walked into the kitchen with both hands full of glasses and tumblers, a few of them slipped away to the floor. A few moments later he staggered in with four large platters in his arms, only to watch helplessly as a large stack of plates by the sink wavered and then buckled in the middle, sending a cataract of crockery and food scraps dashing to the tiles. He slammed the platters down on the counter, cracking the bottom one, and yanked open the cabinet door for some soap. But this door, which had dutifully opened and closed to the man so many times before, flew off its hinges and swung down awkwardly, with the sharp metal corner cutting across his abdomen as he threw the door up against the wall. Günter shouted and clutched the wound, and when he felt how wet it was, he made straight for the parlor shouting, "Nein, nein, nein!" between his teeth.

By the following weekend, however, a new level of harmony existed among relatives and friends. The greatest object of concern was Clara, about whom everyone feared, without saying so, that she would relapse even deeper into her world of sadness. So, as often happens when people do not see what they expect to see, it took everyone several days to begin to relate to the woman the way she now undoubtedly was. She brought tea and sandwiches to Günter every afternoon and had even given Junilde her own bedroom to stay in while her foot was healing. Her sister-in-law was most able to accept this new person named Clara Jepsen, mainly because it was another Jette Ulov that did the accepting. Jette's serenity was still there, even much of the naïveté. Yet no one was quite sure how to react when one afternoon she escorted

Ole Torbeck, the architect, around the house for a sizable estimate on redoing several rooms, including removing the entire conservatory to make way for a new wing. The next day she spoke to Günter at length about arranging for an exhibition of all his available work and then sent off several letters of invitation to the wealthiest art patrons in Sjaeland. She also purchased a handmade china cabinet to house the porcelain that Birte and Jens had generously donated. Jorgen was very happy to have Junilde in the house. They both felt more at ease with each other amid the activity and generosity of everyone around them. Jorgen established a dutiful regimen of study and writing in the morning and early afternoon, and spent the rest of the day reading to Junilde and working in the garden. Occasionally one could notice him pause over whatever he was doing and tilt his head upward with a gentle smile. One time Günter watched this habit commence while the young man was standing by the mantelpiece, and the servant hurried over and took up the crystal vase that was right at his elbow. But Jorgen only laughed and gave Günter a gentle thump on the head with his book. The delicacy of his manner and the evenness of his temperament was a delight to everyone, and naturally enough it was all ascribed to his coming marriage. Junilde never asked him to explain the outcome of his torment. In later years, she often felt that she found the answer in the scar on the sole of her left foot.

Three Sundays following Jorgen's birthday dinner, Herr Torben Nielsen delivered his sermon on "Expectations of the Unknown." He had worked on it for several days, and he had full twelve pages of written manuscript in his hand as he ascended the pulpit in the hot and stuffy church. But when he opened out the sheets in front of him and looked around at the many silent faces in the pews, he felt a rush of abandonment such as he had never before experienced, although he had certainly read about it. It was as though all his intellectual labor no longer made that labor necessary. He gathered up his sheets again and turned them over. He smiled out at his congregation and began to speak. And as he spoke, it was rather to pluck the dangling fruit than to describe the ponderous upward movement of the sap:

"My friends, I have often found myself waiting for something. I have often stood in this pulpit and talked to you, or quoted from the Scriptures, in anticipation of some ultimate insight that would render all uncertainties as but silly excuses for continuing to indulge the lower appetites. Indeed, all indulgence is not without its excuse. And the most common excuse is that we do not know. We have no certainty. We have no specific knowledge of what the Lord wishes from us, and we have not the understanding or the will to ask Him. We are left with emptiness, with nothing—but a nothing so great that to allow it to remain would create a terror as loud and uncompromising as the voice of God Himself. And so the familiar is placed before us. We live and move among what we know. And though it be dreadfully small, the familiar is also dreadfully safe. It is the shelter from which we poke out our heads and pray that God will someday come down and build His house next door to ours. Then we need but dash across the road to Him.

"But we all know such reassurances are only a fiction. So why anticipate a fiction? My own anticipation has taught me something different. Many times I have fervently desired during the course of my sermons that an angel of the Lord would invade my body, as we ourselves would don an overcoat, and continue to speak and indicate in my place, while I simply watched the movement of arm and mouth, declaring His, and not my own, humble sentiments. Such undeniable certainty would give me the greatest comfort, yes, comfort and strength. I would be strong. I would be silent witness to the miracle within. I would have my certainty.

"But, my friends, it does not happen that way. Ah, but wait now! What is it that does not happen this way? The entrance of the angel? Nay, but who can say that? How can we ever know for sure who is speaking whenever our tongue or pen wishes to engage another's attention? Is it the case that we ponder every idea, every observation, and every possible way of elucidating it before it passes through our lips? When we touch the truth with our speech, are we giving up what is ours, or are we not more declaring what belongs to all? Who always knows what he will say before he says it? Who ever knows? But here we come to the kernel of my real objection. Intervention of the angel may well occur, but it does not bring what I described. It does not bring certainty. It does not yield the satisfaction of a fifty-year old brandy, wherewith we may idle by the hearth in winter in our stocking feet and nod into its vapors. Quite the contrary. It shatters everything familiar and exposes us to the emptiness that was always there, but wherein we had before only heard our own echoes. Uncertainty, my friends, is the highest wisdom. Not to know forces one to be. The explorer yearns, against the judgment of his sober faculties, to voyage into deeper and deeper waters and to enter jungles and mountains that, by their very mystery, yield up the giddy tremors in his breast that become the only purpose of his life. We do not want to know. The more we study, the more we are remorseless in our search for precision, the more we find ourselves suspended over an abyss. And from such a height we may truly look with compassion upon those below us who consider what is knowable a refuge. Whenever we are sure of something, we no longer need it.

"I ask you all to consider what I say to you now. I ask you to expect, to desire, to seek the unknown. I ask you to die. Did not our great Teacher and Savior do this? What solace could He find on the cold hillside of Gethsemane as He offered His pain to the silent darkness above Him, with silent disciples at His feet? What answer spoke out of that darkness to rebuke the wish to take His cup that was audible enough to let Him bleed with ease? No, my friends, the bright star burns in the void, and those of us within the void seek its light and not its complaining.

"So you see how absurd it would be to consider uncertainty an excuse for diligence and hard labor. Where most we feel unsure, there must we turn. Where most we feel certain of our grasp, there must we let go. Let us rise now and pray, and ask the angels not for children or lovers or meat or land but for the strength to embrace what is before us now. It is not certainty, but it is here."

It seemed to Torben that the congregation stood up rather slowly for the prayers and hymns that followed. He had perspired a great deal during his sermon, and he was only too glad to get out into the cool air after the service. He stood by the front gate and nodded hello to people as they emerged from inside. He had expected questions and comments about what he had said, and so he found himself turning over various answers in his mind. But no one mentioned it at all. No one even stopped to chat with him about anything. Many people answered his nod and smile with one of their own, and politely walked off. The minister noticed whenever he spoke to someone—as when he expressed to Lotte Kuhlmann his admiration for her new white dress—that they would stop and listen to him, and then continue on their way at the first pause in the conversation. Torben was more relieved than disturbed by this perception. He had spoken a great deal, he was tired, and he had, to his satisfaction at least, made amends for the evening with Jorgen in the garden.

Ever since that moment Torben had considered it an obligation to preach on a theme that related to Jorgen's experience. Yes, Jorgen's experience. Herr Nielsen had not heard anything that night. At first he had grown silent because he thought he had recognized Kire's voice among the crowd on the other side of the field. He was still quite fond of Kire, and it pained him to see her yet unmarried and carrying on with so many different men.

But he had felt the depth of his own selfishness when he looked again at the young man's anxious expression and then immediately realized the opportunity for ridding Jorgen forever of that strange obsession. And so that had passed. But unfortunately the good minister was now left with his own torment. He did not feel guilty about deceiving Jorgen; he did not even brood too often over what Kire could have been doing that night. But something had changed. That he did not know what it was disturbed him the more and had compelled him to read and study and write as he had not done for many years. The result of all that effort was indeed a brilliant essay in its own right, but Torben was quite relieved to have abandoned it in favor of more spontaneous words. He felt that somehow they had almost equaled the suffering Jorgen had been through.

He wandered through the park for a while and reached his favorite tavern by a circuitous route. Many people were sitting on benches in the full sun. One man with a red scarf around his neck was leaning up against the wall next to the tavern entrance, idly blowing clouds of smoke into the air from his big pipe. Torben said hello to him. The man did not answer. Torben started to enter the tavern, but for some reason he found himself hesitating. Inside it was cool and dark. There was the thick smell of beer and tobacco. Many people were speaking at once. The minister stood at the threshold and looked inside for a long time. He looked again at the man with the pipe. The man was chewing on the stem and seemed to be murmuring to himself. Torben looked all around him and saw that everyone, both inside the tavern and out in the sun, everyone was talking.

"Maybe it is always this way," he said, half out loud. He went inside and drank a pint of beer without speaking to anyone. Then he went home.

That evening a messenger delivered to the Nielsen residence a formal invitation card, printed on hand-made paper, announcing a private exhibition of the paintings and drawings of Günter Roos. Marte was most impressed that Torben did not argue when she asked him how much available spending money they had.

That day at the Ulov's was a memorable one. The parlor, the large sitting room and part of the library were all transformed into a modest-sized art gallery. All the drawings were mounted on stiff gray paperboard with matching silver frames, while the seven large oils were all richly displayed in gilded and carved frames, each one appropriate to the subject it contained. Everything had been labeled by Jette in simple, elegant calligraphy, and she had devoted the better part of two days to seeing that all the pictures were hung in the most attractive manner. Jens and Birte and Junilde passed around hors d'oeuvres and served wine to the guests. Günter greeted everyone at the front door with Jette, while Jorgen and Clara escorted them around the rooms. The artist at first seemed a little embarrassed in his blue suit and black shoes, but as more and more people arrived and the compliments and congratulations increased, he was eventually beaming with a well-restrained pride. Fru Ulov also became a bit anxious upon the unexpected arrival of Georg Mannheim. His first remarks to Jette were to complain rather loudly about the way Günter's two landscapes were placed at opposite ends of the same room. There was a tense pause, and then he laughed and said it did not matter much, because he would certainly do them better justice when they were hanging in his own parlor. At this, the entire gathering seemed to rise up several notes on the scale of delight and other promises of purchase from among the crowd soon followed.

Throughout the afternoon Jorgen and Torben exchanged glances many times. The minister appreciated the looks of gratitude that he received, but also felt uncomfortable about seeming to share an understanding that he did not possess. Once everyone had been served food and drink, and the party seemed to move along on its own momentum, Jorgen slipped away from the guests and came up to Torben in the hallway with two glasses of champagne.

"Let's toast to new beginnings, Herr Minister."

"Yes, with pleasure. Who could have dreamed of such success, eh?"

"Oh, but the success will only be complete if we manage to sell you one of those horses."

"Never mind. Marte bought the whole set."

"Wonderful! Let's ring glasses again." After a pause, Jorgen went on, "I heard you created rather a controversy with your sermon last Sunday."

"People have spoken to you about it, then?"

"Yes, yes, as people always do. We cannot expect others to understand what they have never experienced, can we?" He looked at Torben and winked.

The minister looked into his smiling face. "I suppose not," he said rather hesitantly.

Jorgen now became more serious. "No, Herr Minister, do not misunderstand what I mean. You taught me something very precious that evening in the garden. I knew you had not heard the music. After the tolling of the church bell, the sounds had ceased completely inside my own head, and the moment of clarity that followed helped me see what you were really trying to do, and why. You did something for me when I needed it most. You gave me encouragement when I hardly deserved it. You did what was most difficult for you to do. However small it may have seemed to you, the lesson for me proclaimed itself as loud as an entire orchestra blaring between my ears. After those few minutes in the darkness, I knew what I had to do. Let the music come or go as it pleases, it is time for me to serve as you are serving and to stop fighting what I cannot understand." Torben seemed to want to object to some of this, but Jorgen quickly raised an open hand. "No, Herr Nielsen, it is all right. After all, what is a hint of eternity worth without its appropriate gesture in time?"

Herr Nielsen swallowed the last of his champagne and gazed into the room of happy people. "And the harps?" he asked.

Jorgen looked into the room as well. "Yes, the harps. Behold the strings."

They both watched their friends and acquaintances for several minutes. Günter, notepad in hand, was explaining his technique to a group of his new patrons. Jette and Birte stood by the window and confided together about some of their visitors. Clara was holding Herr Mannheim by the arm. The gentleman finished telling a few people one of his clever stories, and she laughed and leaned against his shoulder. At one point Junilde caught Jorgen's eye. She smiled and went into the library.

Jorgen finished his champagne as well. "Excuse me, Herr Nielsen," he said and walked off. Torben continued to watch the party from a distance. After a time he began to consider what such a scene would look like in one of Günter's paintings, but concluded that too much detail could never explain what he was feeling.

One Sunday morning three months later found a happy German artist in the front pew of Herr Nielsen's morning service. Günter had been overwhelmed by the success of the exhibition. Everything except two drawings had been sold. His renewed confidence had prompted him to devote much more time to his art than to his household responsibilities. However, since Jette and Clara were both far more self-reliant these days, and since the workmen had begun tearing away the conservatory, the man's services and meals were not greatly missed. At the same time Günter could not help but remember the conversation that had taken place at Jorgen's birthday dinner. He had begun to feel a little guilty about his success and now considered it prudent not to forget the respect due to the higher powers who gave him what he longed for.

Torben did not notice the artist among the congregation. When it came time for his sermon, the minister stood at the lectern and fumbled over his papers for several minutes. There were a few polite coughs and a little whispering. Günter kept his eyes fixed on Torben. Two boys in the back row began whispering rather loudly and kicking their feet against the bench. A bald-headed man turned around and told them to keep quiet. "You keep quiet!" a youthful voice shouted back at him. Everyone turned in his direction. Many of the older women gasped. The bald-headed man leapt across the stalls and grabbed one of the youths by the hair. "I'll teach you to shout in church!" the man bellowed, and began beating the boy on the back. People shouted for the man to stop. A tall blonde man leapt up and punched him in the face. He let go of the boy and, with a scream of rage, threw his arms around the man's neck and dragged him to the ground. Now several men poured into the aisle and tried to stop the fight. Some of the children started crying. Someone knocked over a basket of coins from the previous collection, and the metal shower was followed by several furtive hands reaching out and stuffing coins into their pockets. Then one of the pews was knocked over. The women screamed, the men argued, and chaos reverberated from one end of the church to the other, like the crashing of ocean waves.

Two people in the church were not affected by all this ruckus. Torben stood perfectly still and gazed up at the ceiling with a gentle smile on his lips. Günter, who was completely oblivious to the rumbling in the pews and the shouts of the congregation behind him, continued to wait patiently for the sermon to begin. He marveled at the minister's serene expression, so much so that he considered making a quick drawing of him on the back page of one of the missals. And then, that thought made the artist realize that at this moment the good minister looked not unlike a certain bronze statue, a sketch of which now hung over the bed of Herr and Fru Jorgen Ulov.

The Poem

for Eric

The Poem

"I...." "I MUST TELL YOU TWO A STORY," the man without a jacket interposed. I call him the man without a jacket because he was dressed as though he should have been wearing one: cuff links, tie tack, vest, Italian shoes. But he was not. "If only to season your discussion. This story is about a poet. A poet who visits a small town."

The bartender and I had been arguing the significance of public opinion. I had described a meeting of our philosophical society last evening, where, after much debate, we concluded that there is only individual understanding and that the apparently unified voice of the many was but an approximation of personal judgments. "But," the bartender had exclaimed, "you all agreed! So what do you call that?" "Agreed approximately. Agreed approximately," I replied in exasperation. It was here that I was stopped by the other man. My argument was well-formed though, and after the man without a jacket's anecdote, I intended to rush right back to the defense of the individual ego.

"Is this a joke?" the bartender asked. It was obvious that he was hoping it were not a joke. He was drying a set of tumblers with a clean cloth, his back resting against the mirror. He was portly and balding and looked stereotypically unreflective—for a bartender, I mean—but he was good-natured and knew how to listen.

"Of a sort. It is a joke of a sort," our storyteller agreed. He and I were the only patrons on this midweek afternoon, and, along with the bartender, we at once achieved an informality that strangers, unrestrained by the conventions of the many, can do with surprising ease.

"A joke need not have a punch line," I offered. "When an apparent truth is turned upside down by a real truth—that is humor."

The bartender chuckled. "What's a real truth?"

"Oh, but this story has a punch line," the man without a jacket stopped us again. He took a sip from his glass and began. "There was this poet. A young guy. He stopped over in this small American town out West. It was in the fall. He stayed with friends—a couple, no children—who gave him a small room at the top of their house. As his friends both worked during the day, the poet was able to breakfast, read, and, of course, write in peace. The poet liked it like this. He had his days to himself, he worked, and then in the evening his friends would return and they would all eat and drink and laugh, or sit by the fire and share stories, or go into town to the theater."

"Was this guy independently wealthy?"

"No, I don't believe he was. I don't actually know too many other details about him except that he liked to go for walks in the morning and that he had red hair. After his walk he would start right in with pen and paper, work until lunch time, then have a bite and go back to it till about four."

"Kept regular, proper hours," the bartender said approvingly, putting away the glass and taking up another. "I wonder if poets feel more free just because they don't get paid. They keep to the clock, but, no money, no trouble." The glass squeaked as it turned through the cloth in his hand.

"I don't think poets feel more free necessarily," I said. "Money or no money. If they feel obliged to write, then they are caught up in responsibilities just like anyone else. The difference is that the responsibilities come from within, from what they feel they need to express. And maybe such responsibilities are more urgent than a boss or a business contract. You can always tell people to go to hell, but you can't tell yourself that."

"Responsibilities of spouse and family come from within."

"No."

"We could argue these subtleties all afternoon," the man without a jacket stopped us again, "for there is a lot to be said for and against." He and I finished our glasses and the bartender refilled them. We both pushed some money forward, but the bartender waved us off. "This one's for the poet," he said, filling himself half a mug. He nodded at the storyteller, who took a sip and continued.

"So what happened was that the first morning, after he was all settled into his new apartment, he said goodbye to his friends, had his breakfast and went for a stroll. As he was unfamiliar with the area, he decided to walk toward the town center and then wander down a few side roads. Now this town was small, you see, in the country. It was not at all like the city here. The main road was paved, but the rest were gravel or dirt. Everything was built of wood. The few commercial buildings were clustered together on one or two streets. The rest were private homes, spread far apart with many pine trees and bushes separating each from each. Like I said it was autumn, so the smells of pine and earth were particularly sweet. The poet walked past the shop windows, looking in here and there to see what people were doing. Once in a while someone would meet his gaze."

"Are you the poet?" the bartender asked.

"No—no, no. This story is a kind of joke, like you said before. Not my autobiography."

"The poet's hair was red," I confirmed.

"Anyway, the poet wandered off down one of the gravel side roads. He saw the occasional house, with a vehicle or two in the drive and a dog or a few cats on the porch. He walked by slowly, but without much lingering over details. He really exhibited little curiosity or surprise over anything. It was often said of him that he looked as though he already knew what he was seeing. Sort of like someone was telling him just a moment beforehand what he was going to see next."

"The Muse," said the bartender.

"No, the Muse is not like that," I put in. I cannot say why this tale, which up to that point said little, aroused so much opinionating in me. In any case, I did not resist it. "The Muse is the feeling that leads you on to create. Something that lets you dare to follow the images that come into your mind. It is always a risk. Like jumping off a high dive. Or going mad. Why follow an internal image? It could well be a psychosis. The Muse is not a voice or a maiden in filmy costume. If the poet does not use the images that come his way, they disappear at once. There is then no feeling of an 'other'."

The man without a jacket seemed to approve of my words. "To define the Muse of poetry, you must use poetry. It is its own definition. I like what you say, but I never thought of it as entering into this side of the poet's character. He just was that way. A bit impassive. But not all poets are like that. I have always preferred the more spontaneous artist, the one who is surprised by everything, who sees everything as new—even his third round." He nodded at the bartender and pushed his empty glass forward. The bartender obliged. "Such artists are usually more sociable. The poet I'm telling you about was a quiet one. If he was surprised, he did not show it."

"That brings to mind an interesting image," I said, responding to the fellow's last remark. "We can't paint the poet's internal world, so we have to infer it from externals—which is really more exciting. The inner world remains a secret, the unknown, and what we have instead is a picture of this guy walking down the road or sitting at his attic window writing under a dim pool of light. Or the surprised smile of the sociable artist, as you say. That interests me more. When, after the party, the poet dons his coat, looks about the room and waves farewell, what does he feel that we do not? Really curious." I finished my second glass and the bartender refilled it. He refilled his own as well and remarked, "He may not have feelings any different from you or me. He may just be better at describing them."

"These are things to discuss, curious things," the man without a jacket said. He paused to be sure he had regained our attention and then resumed. "That first day the poet managed to get himself a little lost. He followed a walking path into the woods in a direction that he thought would bring him back to the main road and near his home. But after a meander of about twenty minutes, he found himself in the yard of one of the houses he had passed earlier. Without much ceremony, he cut through the yard and back to the road. As he passed the front porch, a dog barked at him and leapt at its chain. This brought out the lady of the house, who quieted the dog and asked the stranger what he was doing there. 'Losing and finding,' the poet said, 'losing and finding.' And he continued on his way.

"The woman was nonplussed but made no answer. That evening she told her husband and family about the encounter, more as idle conversation than as suspicion or complaint. I think it was the lack of an explanation that made her talk about it."

"Silence begets words," I said. I was about to follow this up, but the amused expression of my two companions stopped me. "Right," I yielded and became a listener again.

"The next day the poet went into the town center again and chose another side road to explore. I say 'explore' figuratively because he did not really explore things. He just walked for about an hour and returned home. Each day following he developed a slightly different itinerary, though being somewhat a creature of habit, and being unwilling to consume too much time away from his pen, he was seen most of the time in the same places by the same people."

"You would think, though, that he might have been up to something," the bartender said. "People usually have motives."

"Yes, precisely," the man without a jacket smiled, obviously pleased with this conclusion. "That is just what happened. The townspeople began to wonder if this character was not 'up to something.' The first time private suspicion became public chattel was when that woman on the front porch was at market one morning. She saw the figure with red hair on the far side of the street just turning the corner. She pointed him out to the fruit seller, who remarked, 'Yes, he comes around almost every morning. Seems to like my tomatoes. Doesn't buy much else.' But the woman, wishing to make more of the moment, told him her story of the man's intrusion, with enough embellishments to arouse the fruit seller to say, 'Well, I'll spread the word. Let's watch him. We'll soon know if something's wrong.'

"So the word spread. You can imagine how quickly. The whole town was soon as aware of the poet's presence as we would be of the next person who entered this bar. They all watched him a little more closely from then on, but he himself didn't seem to mind. No, his behavior didn't change at all."

The man without a jacket paused to drink from his glass. I watched the entrance to see if another client would enter. It would have been an appropriate moment for it to happen.

"He didn't change. People, and you know how funny people can get, were afraid to talk to him. Before, it had hardly occurred to them to talk to him. But now that rumor was in the air, and he the object of it, they were afraid. It became an adventure to watch this character, to watch the way he purchased things, where he kept his money, what he wore, the quality of his voice and all that. Ridiculous really, but they were now in total fascination. Everything he did was unusual. Everything he said seemed to have a double meaning. Everywhere he went people imagined clandestine encounters, a rendezvous with a woman, or smugglers or horse thieves. Anything. When the shopkeepers saw him turn down a lane, they assumed that a few dozen yards out of their sight would be the answer to the secret, while that few dozen yards down the lane an old man or old woman would watch the figure pass, assuming that he had either come from the secret or was heading toward it.

"There was talk. Much, much talk. They knew where the poet lived. They respected his friends as upright members of the community. A few of the bolder ones even managed to find out from the couple where the poet came from, what else he had done for a living, how long he intended to stay, and so on. But knowing these things—and I assure you eventually everybody knew them—did not satisfy. They felt the poet was doing something, or that he knew something that no one else knew, not even the generous friends he lived with. So, with their curiosity eventually at white heat, and the poet's daily wanderings continuing with relentless consistency, a few of these bolder ones decided to follow through with the only possible course of action. They went to the sheriff."

I had my glass to my lips and lost some brew for laughing. "So this is your punch line," I said, soaking up my accident with a few cocktail napkins. I pushed my empty glass and my money forward and insisted to the bartender that I pay for the next round. While pouring them out, he said frowning, "I would never be that suspicious. Never. I don't care what people do."

"But it isn't what he did," I said. "It's what he didn't do."

"What didn't he do?"

I hesitated, not really knowing where that dialectic had led me. I looked to the man without a jacket for help, who nodded and said, "Let's find out." He took a long swallow from his fresh glass and went on. "The sheriff was also bold. Sheriffs are paid to be bold. He didn't really care about the poet's daily walks either. He had passed him on the street several times and had always been greeted with a pleasant hello. He had maybe been among the least curious of the community. But he was paid to act for others, and so he did. He sat in his patrol car one morning near the poet's residence and waited for him to come out. A few townspeople were gathered across the way trying to look inconspicuous. A contradiction in terms, of course. Eventually the poet came out of the house, and the sheriff got out of his car. The figure approached the sheriff, the sheriff nodded good morning;

the poet returned the hello and continued on his way. The sheriff glanced at the crowd, who were all silence and anticipation. He quickly turned round and called out, 'Hey, Poet, I'd like to ask you something.' The poet stopped and turned. The sheriff came up to him. He was quick about it. 'I was just wondering, and some of the folks here were wondering,' he made a brief gesture in the direction of the crowd, 'what you are doing.' 'Doing?' the poet asked and looked himself over to see if something in his dress had aroused the question. 'Doing? I am going for a walk.' 'May I ask where?' 'I'm not sure yet,' the poet replied, 'just around.' The sheriff was a trifle confused. 'How could you not be sure? I mean, either you're going somewhere or you're not.' 'Yes,' the poet said, 'that's true. I am going for a walk.' The sheriff did not reply, so the other turned and walked off."

The man without a jacket had amused us by putting on voices for the two characters. ("Get you on TV," the bartender said.) "The sheriff watched him retreat into the distance until he had disappeared from view. He did not wish to face the townspeople just then, so he went straight to his patrol car and drove off. All who witnessed the scene had to wait two days to hear about it. Ridiculous." The fellow chuckled and sipped his ale. I did the same. The bartender dried the last of the glasses and knelt down to stock the refrigerator with beer and soda. We were all silent for a while.

"Before you finish," the bartender's voice came from below where he was working. "Let me tell you about a conversation I overheard last weekend. I don't know why, but it seems somehow related to all this. My wife and I were having lunch in a coffee shop downtown. She was busy with the crossword, so I just ate and stared out the window. 'Look at those crowds,' a voice said. I looked up and saw a man of middle age in the next booth, apparently talking to himself. 'Look at them. People crossing the street, walking here and there, sitting in cafés, in their cars, wandering in and out of shops. If you were somehow able to stop each single person and ask who they were and where they were going, what would you discover? Even if people told you everything that they did throughout their entire life right up to the moment when they arrived there in front of you, what would that explain?' I waited to see if the ketchup bottle would talk back to him. But then I heard this other voice say, 'I'm not with you. Just tell me what you mean.' It was the voice of an old man. He was sitting opposite the fellow, but he must have been pretty short. I supposed that he was the guy's father. The first man said, 'The human body is finite, but it contains an infinity of cells. One galaxy contains an infinity of stars. This crowd is finite, but it holds an infinity of moments.' 'Moments?' the voice on the bench was puzzled. 'Moments. Like I say, go up to any individual out there and talk to them. How many moments of experience does one of those people hold? The finite stream of time, be it a day, a week, or just this afternoon, moves at right angles to the infinity of human experience. When you meet a new friend, your life changes completely. Even the momentary exchange of eye contact between passersby can change their entire day.' 'You and your dreams, and your eye contact,' the old man said. 'Miriam tells me all about it. You have to get so friendly with every stranger you meet?' I stopped listening after that," the bartender stood up, "since I could see it was really the guy's father-in-law."

We all laughed. Then I said, "Curious of that fellow to apply metaphysics to Saturday shopping. We glance out our window and see a person walk by. That is one moment, the so-called cross-section of time. But if you were to follow that person for several hours, I am sure time would reveal all. The essential person would be identified. And that is finite, too."

The bartender laughed. "Someone just went by out there. If you hurry, you might be able to catch him."

Our banter stirred the man without a jacket. "This, gentlemen, is where my story continues. People did just that with our poet. Since direct confrontation did not work, they followed him. For five days in a row a different person followed him on his morning walk, and at the end of the week they compared notes."

"Of course they found nothing," the bartender said.

"Of course. But people don't like 'nothing.' Eventually a few of them, then little by little the entire community, got up their nerve to ask the poet what he was doing. 'What are you doing there, poet?' someone would ask. And he would say, 'I am going for a walk.' Then the fruit seller came round to querying, 'What are you doing, poet?' and he would reply, 'Buying some of your tomatoes.' The antique dealer would ask, 'What are you doing?' and as quickly had the answer, 'Looking at your antiques.' This went on for some time. Then people grew tired of asking, though they never grew tired of the mystery. The antique dealer, for instance, tried looking at his antiques, and the fruit seller once bought a bag of tomatoes from another grocer, just to see what would happen. But nothing ever happened except the thing itself."

"What was the end of it all?" I asked.

"That was the end. He stayed until the first snows and then moved on. I believe he went to Italy. He wrote his hosts occasionally, and about a year later sent them a collection of poems that he was able to get published. Many of them had been written during his stay there."

"Did any of the people in the town read his poems?" the bartender asked.

"Oh yes, certainly, and enjoyed them. There was one lyric that was a favorite of theirs. They used to recite it formally at autumn gatherings, like dances or Thanksgiving meals, and informally among themselves. It went like this." The man without a jacket hopped off his stool and faced us with some degree of gravity. This prompted me to adjust my posture and give him full ear. The bartender leaned back against the mirror. Then the man without a jacket clasped his hands together before him and recited the few stanzas with great feeling.

I do not know, and I will probably never know, how words arranged in a certain way can arouse so much more than words. Arouse feeling. And silence. I listened to those lines, I reached but could not grasp, and at last I let them work on me and engender what they would.

And as he spoke, I somehow saw myself under a willow tree by a lake. I look out upon the lake and bright sunlight shimmers on its happy surface. Across the way are lush grasses and trees with ripe fruit. There is a warm haze in the air. Men and ladies linger on the grass and wander along the white gravel path. I hear their distant laughter. Under the willow tree it is cold. The wind whips the supple branches that occasionally sting my eyes. The ground is black and hard. My toes are numb.

I often have these pictures whenever I remember those lines recited by the dapper man with no jacket. That day a tear started and I brushed it away. I still brush them away. What sorrow, or was it a joy, led you to these phrases, my poet? Dear God, I wanted to know. My heart burned bright, and I knew it was so for my two companions. No one spoke for several minutes.

"Could you write that out for me?" the bartender asked at last.

"Certainly." The man without a jacket reflected for a few minutes. "You know, many years later, after a recitation of this poem, it became a traditional joke in that town for two people to exchange the following: 'I say there, what is a poem?' 'Why, a poem is a poem.' 'Ah, so it is.' 'Yes, so it is.' Yes, they were always proud that that poet had passed some days with them, though they never quite understood what he was doing."

The bartender started as if out of a dream and took up my glass to refill it. "A beer is a beer," he said.

"So it is," said the storyteller, paying for it, "so it is."

The Stage

The Stage

THERE IS A STAGE. The curtain rises and the actors come forth. The opening speeches are often uninteresting, or at least seem that way. Some of the actors have memorized their opening speeches quite thoroughly. So sometimes, despite the monotony, you notice those first few words. This is especially the case when the curtain has risen, the actors begin moving and talking and, just before the first speech comes out, you wonder if it will be the same or not. So you listen. And so it is the same. It's very effective.

There are many different kinds of actors, as you might expect. Some much more skilled than others. Some, though not many, with a flair for improvisation. Some are women, some men. They say many things to each other: profound, silly, rude, obscene, secretive, shocking, boring, obsequious, disdainful. They know what they're saying. Well, I should say, to a certain extent. Actors do know what they're saying; I'm not questioning that. It's just that, you know, as the lines are constantly being repeated over and over again, I'd have to say that they know them, but maybe they don't know them.

It's like this. Say the following out loud: "Please take my hand—I love you." (That's right, say it—right now. Don't bother reading further until you do.)

Okay, now say this: "Go eat your cereal in the kitchen, so we don't have to look at you!" (Come on, come on! Whisper it if you think someone is listening.)

All right, one more. Now say this: "My tennis shoes are too tight, but the air is really fresh." (You must be getting used to this already.)

So that's all, really. But the catch is, if you were to put down this story every couple of minutes and say one of those sentences aloud again, what do you think would happen? This is what I mean. They know, but they don't know.

I must say, the lines are usually very well delivered. Incredible. Well, no, it is credible, but nevertheless impressive. When a certain actor encounters a certain actress say, about one third into the play, you can see the drama building, the looks, the questioning, the fears, or whatever and then the lines. His line. Her line. His line. Her line. His line. Her line. His line. Her line. His line. Pause. His line. Her line. His line. Her line. Pause. End of scene.

Perfectly accurate. During their apprenticeship, most actors have trouble with many of their lines. Sometimes the trouble is that they can't remember them. Whenever this occurs, some of their senior thespian counterparts will whisper to them, or maybe even poke, maybe even shout the required phrase at the necessary moment. It takes a few dozen whispers, but only about four pokes, and maybe only one or two well-timed shouts, for the new recruit to begin snapping out his lines with animated precision. You do find cases, I must admit, where, even when the actor finally gets his lines right remarkably well every time, the shouting and the poking doesn't stop. Actors get used to that. Actually, it becomes incorporated into their repertoire. I've noticed many an original line or dialogue or even school of tragedy develop from one sound wallop across the head or a couple of ear-splitting shrieks from some impatient veteran.

Actually, though, the main trouble with new actors remembering their lines is that they don't know what they mean. This can become very complicated sometimes. A new actor learns his lines, seems to get through them fairly well for a while, but then seems to lose the grasp of it all, or, shall we say, the momentum. He doesn't quite see why he must say or do this after they say or do that. He knows it works. But why can he not do something else instead—like touch their face maybe, or point to the river, or, for that matter, tell them to go eat their cereal in the kitchen. This can be very difficult for some actors, a hurdle that many of them never quite overcome. Usually, they either carry on saying their lines rather unconvincingly until the customary responses and dénouements compel them to forget their incredulity; or they stop coming on stage at all. They don't forget the lines though. So at least they know, to a certain extent, what is going on out there.

There have been various theories presented now and again about the right way to handle this problem. Many actors are convinced—and point to their own careers as an illustrative testimonial—that the best thing to do is learn all the lines, gestures, scenes, movements as thoroughly as possible, and the meaning of it all will reveal itself. Once you have done a performance enough times, well, then it's all quite clear after all. One could say it is the privilege of seniority to be able to follow a drama through from beginning to end and know, by means of experience and repeated effort, what will happen next, and why.

You could call this the traditional school of thought. It has many adherents, perhaps even a majority. There are other theories, though, some of them rather more interesting. There is the pure memory school of thought, for example, that considers any notion of meaning in the play or understanding of lines and gestures totally irrelevant. For these actors, the most important thing is memorization, perfection, absolute precision in every action and word. And that's all. Admittedly, people from this school are among the finest actors on the stage. They are very convincing, if for no other reason than that nothing holds them back. They've learned their lines, they know what's coming, and they forge ahead. There is another branch of this particular school, by the way, that also believes in memorization, but not necessarily in demonstrative acting. The underlying principle here is that once you know everything that's going to happen, there is no need to expend all one's energy on doing the same bit over and over again. These are usually the people who become stage-hands, dressers, make-up people, you know.

Another school, on the other hand, firmly believes in the notion of questioning the lines, even the plot. Such actors are absolute renegades. The annoying thing is that many of them are very good and learn all their lines very quickly. But they develop annoying habits. They say other people's lines just before they begin them themselves. Whenever they're situated off-stage, either having just finished a scene or preparing to come on again, they stand and jeer at those currently performing, mimicking their gestures to themselves or to some of the others standing by, or sometimes even running on stage and interrupting the entire action. I'm telling you, when there are enough of these misanthropes around, an entire act can end up in a regular free-for-all!

By the way, have you been pausing to say those lines every few minutes? It's no good just repeating them to yourself in your mind. I'm not of the perfect memorization school, to be perfectly frank about it.

There are various types of renegades, and one of them is particularly fascinating. These are the improvisers. Many people are convinced that these particular actors know the director, or the author of the script, because they seem to be able to introduce new themes and new lines with an ease and certainty befitting a real master of the theatre. I myself tend to think that they've been watching the various scenes rather intently for a while before introducing their own material. But it's not necessarily like that, of course, at least not always. Other people are more inclined to think that they just make it up as they go along, somehow managing to shape it into the particular action at hand. It is obviously the case that if you have enough force of character, or if you simply yell loud enough, or grab your partner and compel him to listen to you, a change of scene will take place. But many improvisers are more subtle than that. Some actors feel that the director has actually prearranged the improvisations, so that it is not really an improvisation at all but part of the original script. And then the fun begins. Because the surprise, annoyance, dismay or whatever of the other actors becomes an improvisation of a sort as well. And it works. It works because the other actors could learn their new, unexpected reaction and repeat it next time around; but this is rather ineffective. Instead, more often than not, they simply wait for the next surprise and develop a repertoire of responses, now laughing, now ignoring it, now weeping, whatever they happen to be good at. Some people—indeed some improvisers as well—claim to actually hear the director whispering his new lines to the improviser, which he then passes on into the general action of the play.

It is curious to observe that all these different schools of thought and acting techniques can coexist on the stage. They are all necessary. I'm convinced of that. So much is needed to put on a successful production.

Funny thing about this improvisation stuff. For any actor sensitive enough, it does become a source of wonder as to what is written into the script and what is not. Especially when you are involved in the scene yourself! There was a story going around quite recently about a long-time traditionalist suddenly letting forth the most remarkable stream of profanities for about six minutes before he realized what was going on. It was quite out of character for him, so much so that two perfect memorizationists fainted dead away. This caused quite a commotion, because one of them was carrying a large porcelain doll that shattered into a thousand pieces. One of the renegades then saw his chance and rushed on from stage right to sweep it all up and throw in a few obscene remarks of his own. It was most hilarious!

But you see, was it improvisation, or part of the script? Nobody's quite sure. I suppose this is one of the sublime mysteries that an actor always carries with him. You play the part; you know, and you don't know.

Some actors are better than others. I'm not sure what makes an actor good or bad. They are rather artificial terms much of the time. Many, of course, consider the improvisers to be the best, since they are obviously the most original. But I don't think it's that simple. Some of the traditionalists know a thing or two, and even the perfect memorizationists have their fine moments, though as I said, I'm not partial to them. And there are many other schools. But they all play on the same stage.

Oh, but I haven't yet explained how the play ends, or about the various techniques actors employ for bringing a story to its conclusion. There are, in fact, not very many ways of doing this. One of the most common is to just drop everything. Yes, I'm not kidding, this is an actual method. The moment of realization approaches, the finishing touches to the new manuscript are just about done, that emotional crisis almost reaches fever pitch and then—bang—it goes dark and the curtain falls. Subsequent plays often refer to what happened previously, and sometimes even refer to these special moments that almost just occurred.

But seldom do they elaborate on them or bring to fruition what was only a promise. The promise becomes its own conclusion. Most actors think that that's the way it should be; and well, who knows, maybe it is. I'm not one to argue ad infinitum about it. Another common technique for ending a play is to always end it in the same way. This is easy. Actors are trained to develop a few closing routines, complete with speech, gesture, et cetera; and then, no matter what they happen to be doing when the curtain time approaches, they slowly pause, do their well-rehearsed bit, and down comes the you know what. The only other approach that I've heard about is, for one thing, just that—I've only heard about it. I've never seen it done, although a few times it was rumored that it actually happened when I and many of my friends were there. But I didn't notice it.

The way it's done is simple. The play doesn't end. The actors don't stop acting. The plot thickens, even though the audience thins out. It's hard to prove this because, well, because of one very obvious fact—the curtain goes down. So how do you know what is happening—if anything at all? Some traditionalists and renegades point to the fact (the only fact they both agree to pointing to) that the next play is not totally unconnected to the previous one. In fact, there are many subtle echoes of previous scenes, and sometimes a few blatantly obvious repetitions. But, such a burden to the actor! I am sure that very, very few of them engage in this sort of excruciating labor. To continue on and on, always to play, always to speak, react, explain, convey—it's not real. Or maybe it is. I suppose it would be, come to think of it, if you're actually doing it. Aye, there's the reality. There's the rub. To die, to sleep no more.

Yes, there is a stage. What is this stage? It is very doubtful, Mr. or Ms. or Mrs. Reader, that you have perused more than sixteen lines of this discourse before the wheels of metaphor and hyperbole began cleverly spinning inside your inquisitive little cerebellum. (But hopefully not while you spoke your lines— right?) The stage is not life; I don't know much about that. It is not heaven, or hell, or purgatory, or limbo. I wouldn't know any of those places if I fell over them. And it's certainly not, "All the world". That ain't my line! No, this stage I refer to is that discreet unit of time that we call a day. That's right, a day. Twenty-four hours. Tick tock. The curtain goes up, the day begins, the scene proceeds, often as expected; the main plot unfolds (although I must admit I am very, very seldom informed as to what it is), the climax occurs, the resolution takes place—and the curtain falls. Who needs applause?

What do we do with a day, fellow thespians? Or what does it do to us? I've come to the conclusion that it avails nothing to add them up or to string them together like so many colored beads. No, it just doesn't work for me. It's such an illusion, count- ing time. For instance, I have yet to be convinced that a day is shorter than a week. But that's another matter.

No, I prefer to see it as a stage. Try it yourself. Watch how often the lines come forth with such ease, such distracted elo- quence. Watch for your cues. Or better yet, watch everybody else's. It's the only stage I know of where the actors and the audience can be the same person, even in the same moment. Just imagine that, sitting back and enjoying a particularly gripping moment when the principal character (you) is about to say what he has never said before. Furthermore, it seems to me that herein lies one of the, if you will, cornerstones of improvisation. When you watch it and act it long enough… well, then you can do what you like, can't you? Within reason, of course. Well, maybe without reason.

Is your curtain about to go down now? Or just recently come up? Or is this Act 3, Scene 1? Come on—what's next?!

The Tale of the Sultan's Sentence

The Tale of the Sultan's Sentence

T HE EVENTS IN THIS STORY took place about seven hundred years ago. After I had read the tale, which was included in *A History of Persia After the Time of Christ* by the French historian Binet, and had become gripped with the idea of retelling it for my friends, I came to realize two things: first of all, that I could greatly improve the style and syntax of the translator's rather haphazard prose (in all likelihood, English was not his mother tongue) and secondly that I could remove much extraneous material without seriously harming the main current of the narrative. With this view in mind, then, I have eliminated the digressions relating to the social habits of the people of Tarakin (which in their essential nature are not so different from our own or anyone else's), the explanation of the penal code, the description of tortures used by the soldiers and—I am sure the reader will thank me for this— the description of the sultan's daily toilet. Wherever possible and appropriate, I have also used simpler words and more current forms of expression. As for M. Binet's footnotes on historical events in the Middle East contemporary with this tale, I can only say that, in my own humble, and admittedly biased, opinion, they are irrelevant. What is most touching and instructive about this story is the human side of it, the side that relates to the individual. Seldom, if ever, does a lengthy study of a mass of people, or a society or group, bring us any nearer to understanding the heart of a single person, especially that most enigmatic of all persons, oneself. Besides, from our modern vantage point in the twenty-first century, the student of history would do better consulting someone like Toynbee, who helped bring a true sense of scale to the study of history, as modern science has resurrected it from the rubble of the ages. So let the matter rest at that.

Before I begin to tell the story itself, there is something else I noticed while reading the original version that I wanted to mention here. We all seem to have a profound fascination for the past, profound in the sense that we often consider the past, especially the ancient past, to contain a wisdom that we modern men and women have somehow missed, or have not suffered for sufficiently to acquire. It could be that the great distance at which we stand from historical events five hundred and more years ago persuades us to see only the golden glow on the horizon and conceals from our view the mundane and cruel details fomenting underneath. It could also be that it is only timeless wisdom that survives the ravage of the years and that this wisdom can still instruct us now, because, in relation to ordinary human-cum-animal interests, it appeals to, and dwells among, a world eternal in relation to our own. Whatever the specific psychology of it, we look to the past as our teacher. This is even true of our own individual life. After a few years have gone by, we often understand what went before much more clearly than we did at the time we experienced it. Is the past wiser than the present? It explains little to say that we are the product of our past. We could just as well say that we are the product of our future—some future encounter or enterprise may be beckoning to us right now without our realizing it. But in the future is action only; there is no knowledge there. All knowledge is in the past; all experience is in the present. We might more accurately state that the past is a world above us rather than behind us and that the experiences of they who have preceded us are the language of that world.

But to the story. I will start by summarizing the most important details before turning to Binet's narrative proper. The city of Tarakin in southern Persia was a major center for trade and carpet weaving in the thirteenth century. Almost any merchant traveling to India or to the Mediterranean would stop here to exchange goods or purchase new carpets. Along with the bustling commercial life there also existed, understandably enough, a bustling life of crime as well. Tarakin was replete with thieves of all sorts: highwaymen, smugglers, slave traders, crafty businessmen, pickpockets, every type of practitioner of the dishonest art imaginable, which made the life of the honest trader one of continual peril and frustration. The notoriety of the area eventually prompted a saying that still survives today: "When you go to Tarakin, swallow your purse." I might add, though, that these days the adage refers more to the naïveté of they who flaunt their riches in circumstances that dictate more prudence.

About 12__ Jahid-al-Rajahn became Sultan. This man was the adopted son of Sultan Abir and was curiously the only male of the royal family for a full generation. Both Abir and his older brother Baladhin sired eleven daughters between them. Their sister Jelazza died giving birth to her first child, a son, who only survived his mother by four months. Jahid-al-Rajahn was exceptionally fierce during much of his reign. His ferocity was not that of a barbarian, but rather of a staunchly religious man (which is sometimes much worse). Binet notes that this Sultan seems to have had more of a Protestant Christian mentality than that of a Moslem. There is some truth to this observation, not only because Jahid-al-Rajahn practiced monogamy and lived so austerely, but also because of his almost fanatical desire to eradicate the sin of thievery from Tarakin and indeed the entire southern region. What followed then, when he first came to power, was six years of uninterrupted purges implemented by an elite corps of the Sultan's Royal Guard. Relative peace with the neighboring peoples helped make this action possible. Caravans were painstakingly searched for any illegal merchandise; soldiers wandered through the marketplace and had full authority to arrest and punish anyone even lightly suspected of a crime; merchants were obliged to account in great detail to the financial minister for everything purchased and sold; robbers were in turn ambushed and hunted down in the neighboring valleys; all citizens had to ask permission to travel outside the borders of the kingdom.

And the punishments were severe. Public executions became almost a weekly spectacle in Tarakin. The Sultan had a large arena constructed just south of the marketplace. The populace were not only obliged to attend these gruesome events, but often the heads and bodies of the condemned were left dangling over the north wall of the arena as a perpetual warning to the would-be thieves of the marketplace. Ironically, aside from evoking fear in virtually everyone, the arena eventually came to serve another purpose that worked to the Sultan's advantage. The regular occurrence of seeing men beaten, executed and humiliated satisfied the bloodthirsty urge of the crowd. It became a form of recreation, like the gladiator combats and Christian persecutions of ancient Rome. The people rejoiced almost to the point of ecstasy when a new group of thieves had been apprehended and brought to trial. On the morning of the appointed day merchants either rested idly or sold their goods at reduced prices. Then, after the noonday meal and rest, everyone rushed to this Eastern Coliseum with that fascination for horror that allures all men, no matter what their moral principles might be. It was thus that the public spectacles of justice in the arena of Jahid-al-Rajahn soon became as necessary to the life of Tarakin as its marketplace and its carpets.

The purges of the government proved effective, and crime subsided noticeably in Persia for the first time in almost sixty years. The arena was still active as a center for punishment, but the frequency of the events diminished to only a few times a year. The craving of the townspeople for such entertainments did not subside proportionately however, and, luckily for them, neither did the severity of the Sultan. It was during this time of domestic peace that Jahid-al-Rajahn introduced a new custom for dealing with condemned criminals. All convicted men and women were forced to stand in the arena before all the people of the community, state their name and the nature of their crime—and then decide their own punishment! The psychological pain and suspense generated by this new horror greatly fascinated the spectators. This practice was further enhanced by the presence of the Sultan himself. Whereas he had never previously attended the public executions when they occurred with bloody frequency, he now personally supervised and conducted the "sentencing" of all his victims. A special platform was erected in the center of the arena with a podium facing the royal throne. One by one each prisoner mounted the platform, faced Jahid-al-Rajahn, and sealed his own fate. Throughout these proceedings the Sultan never betrayed the least emotion. He would sit and stare grimly at each individual presented to him, usually with his chin resting on his hand. He would listen impassively to each person's story, whether it was delivered in tones of defiance, self-pity, or despair; and then, after the person pronounced his own sentence of imprisonment, beating, or even death, he would say simply, "So be it."

It is difficult to assess the fear of punishment that now permeated the community of Tarakin because of the Sultan's sentence. This fear was amplified by the fact that everyone knew what had caused him to think of it. They remembered the evening that the royal hunting party approached the city walls at dusk, and they had heard not the triumphant music of bells and cymbals and song, but rather the murderous cry of sorrow coming from the Sultan himself. As the troop unhappily rode through the main gate, people were horrified to see the body of Albahin, the Sultan's sixteen-year old son, lying on a bier with a broken neck. The boy's horse had reared suddenly during the chase, and he was killed the instant he hit the ground. The Sultan tried to hide his tears in his cloak as he galloped through the streets, and he ran directly into the palace and locked himself inside his bed-chamber for three days. He did not emerge or admit anyone to his presence during this time, not even his wife: her attempts to offer him food and solace were met only with rigid silence. Then, on the morning of the fourth day, Jahid-al-Rajahn appeared in the council chamber at the usual hour, cleaned and dressed and betraying no signs of hunger or despair over his past ordeal. However, the Sultan, who ordinarily enjoyed lively conversation and the exchange of witty remarks with his advisors, exhibited a face that was now as silent and distant as a mountain. He nod-ded appreciatively at the condolences of his officers, he listened politely to the reports about the kingdom's problems, both do-mestic and foreign, and then, with this same impassive air, he read out his new decree from a parchment he had been clutching in his hand the entire time: "All criminals will now appear before the sultan and exact their own sentence in just accordance with the nature of their crime and of their own sense of fair retribu-tion to the people of Tarakin, of the Sultan Jahid-al-Rajahn and to themselves..." It went on to describe the particulars already mentioned.

At this point I will quote directly from Binet. What follows here is a description of the sentencing of five men one summer afternoon in July of 12___. This day was remembered long afterward because of the unusual circumstances that surrounded the proceedings and, more importantly, because of what came to light sometime later in connection with this day when the journal of Haladin, the Sultan's chief advisor, was discovered among his papers after both he and the Sultan were killed during Askfahan's uprising. Binet proceeds as follows:

"The day was unspeakably hot, but the crowd was lively and talkative nevertheless. For although there were only five prisoners, two of them were Europeans, an unprecedented occurrence in Tarakin. Usually Western merchants were able to bribe their way out of any embarrassing discovery that the soldiers might make. But this time, either through lack of money or firm resolve on the part of their captors, these two men were thrown into this hostile arena to face the Sultan's unusual sentence. The excited chatter of the crowd did not even subside when the Sultan, Haladin, and others entered the arena and walked across the ground to the royal partition. The Sultan himself seemed unusually preoccupied today. He stared at the ground before him with a heaviness reminiscent of that first day when he had emerged from the silence of his bedchamber. He did not look around at the people in the arena, as was his wont, but conversed only with Haladin.

"Even after Jahid-al-Rajahn was seated, the talk and excitement in the crowd went on for several minutes more. Then the east door opened, and the chatter ceased. Askfahan was the first to emerge, his long dagger thrust into his wide black sash. He led the five prisoners by a long chain that linked each of them at the wrists. Another soldier followed carrying a wooden pole on his shoulder. The small party stopped near the platform and turned to face the Sultan. Haladin rose and prepared to give the opening remarks, while Askfahan unlocked the manacles of the five men. The soldier with the pole walked over to the foot of the steps leading up to the podium.

"The first two prisoners, Aziz and Percleon by name, were well known to the community. They were both merchants and long-time friends, and had won everyone's respect as two of the most honest traders in Tarakin. But just last week they were apprehended trading in false gems; and, when the investigation went further, the royal guard discovered that they had been selling 'diamond' jewelry made of cut glass for over six years. This disclosure shocked most of the people into resentment, and they were now only too glad to see the two men in the arena. Conversely, the third prisoner, Rashin, had always been despised by everyone. Twice he fought duels with and killed two of the noblest young men of the kingdom. Everyone knew that he did this out of spite and jealousy (he was himself an epileptic and had a deformed face) and moreover that he had placed large wagers on these contests and so was well off because of his malice. But last month, when he fought with Surakhan, the gentle son of Tarakin's finest sculptor, he was surprised by the young man's agility and barely escaped with his own life. Since he was, of course, unable to pay his huge wagers, the four merchants who had gambled with him turned him in. Because of this action, they themselves were spared. So likewise, no one felt any sympathy for Rashin.

"Yet despite the infamy of these three men, of the unsuspected criminality of the first two and the detested notoriety of the third, all eyes instead were fixed on the two blond strangers from Central Europe. Although one of the two men stood almost head and shoulders over his comrade, both were muscular in build and stared about with marked defiance. The novelty of their situation must have made them feel light and confident despite their inevitable fate. The taller man appeared particularly calm and self-assured. For several moments, as Haladin prepared to speak, he stared unwaveringly at Jahid-al-Rajahn. The Sultan seemed not to notice this, although he did now and then glance in his direction. The smaller man had a more angry, mocking expression. While Askfahan was unlocking his fetters, he moved his arms about to make it that much more difficult for the soldier. Just before he dropped the chain and returned to his place at the head of the line, Askfahan exchanged a menacing glance with his prisoner.

"As always Haladin began by reading the excerpt from the Sultan's original decree. Then, addressing Askfahan, he said, 'You may lead the first of the accused to the podium.' Askfahan almost absently grabbed Aziz by the arm and nudged him toward the platform. But Aziz, who had stood trembling the whole time biting his lower lip, suddenly threw himself on the ground and started sobbing and kicking about like a wounded boar. Askfahan was unruffled by this, and he surrounded the man in his broad arms and carried him bodily over to the platform. Both soldiers pushed him up the stairs amid his continued sobbing and scream-ing. When he reached the podium, he placed his hands on the railing and stared down at his feet, weeping bitterly. For a few moments the merchant gave no indication that he would say or do anything else. The soldier by the platform ascended a couple of steps, raised the pole over his head, and looked questioningly at the royal partition. Haladin held up his hand to indicate no and then calmly said to the prisoner, 'We are waiting, Aziz.'

"The merchant dried his eyes and looked up at the Sultan. Amid occasional sobs and with a quavering voice, he said the following: 'Sire, it humiliates me to have to stand before you in this way. You know my years of service and all that I have done for you and the people of Tarakin. My innocent error in making an additional profit for my large family surely cannot be of such magnitude that I must be condemned here today.' He stopped and began sobbing again. The Sultan remained unmoved. Aziz looked at him imploringly and wiped his eyes and brow. Still there was no response. Aziz screamed, 'Why must this happen! I sold artificial gems as real diamonds, I kept the money locked away in my house, and I... I...' Again he paused sobbing with his hands covering his face, and then said, 'I must die. So let it be the noose.' The poor merchant swooned and fell to his knees after these last words. Just then the crowd at the eastern end of the arena began shouting with one voice. At first the royal party thought it was because of Aziz's speech, but suddenly they noticed the real reason: Percleon was heading for the low wall beside the gate. Askfahan, who was big and slow, lumbered after him cursing epithets all the while. Three men jumped down from the stands and ran off after the prisoner as well. But Percleon, just as he approached the wall, stumbled and fell clumsily to his hands and knees. He screamed, scrambled to his feet, and tried to leap the wall; but he had not the strength, and soon his pursuers were upon him.

"Everyone was on their feet now, except the Sultan, and shouting at the top of their voices. Askfahan impatiently pushed away the other men and shoved Percleon ahead of him toward the platform. Jahid-Al-Rajahn said something to Haladin, and the minister clapped his hands and shouted for silence. There was much shuffling and murmuring for several minutes. Haladin clapped and called for silence again, and the crowd gradually came to rest.

"Percleon was now on the platform with Aziz. The latter rose and stared at his friend, then at the Sultan's box. When at last he was able to be heard, the Sultan leaned forward and, almost with a look of dejection, said to Aziz, 'So be it.'

"Aziz was now completely broken in spirit, and he left the platform and went into the prisoner's chamber without another sound. Percleon stared after Aziz until Haladin roused him, 'Percleon, turn and face the Sultan, and begin.'

"The man did as he was told and made the following speech in a flat, monotonous voice, 'I have served your highness as devoutly as my friend; and I am sorry beyond words for what we have done. Just now I tried to run from you and from my fate out of blind fear, and I am sorry for this as well. But since I have committed the same crime as my lifelong friend, and since he has chosen death as the only possible retribution, so must I follow him into the netherworld; and so I will die.' The crowd was silent, except for the loud cry of one woman. Everyone knew it was Percleon's wife. The Sultan seemed profoundly moved as well. He bowed his head and said nothing for a few moments. Then he looked up, seemingly brushed away a tear, and said, 'So be it.'

"Percleon calmly descended the stairs and was led away. Then another unusual thing occurred. With characteristic boldness Rashin, not waiting for Haladin or Askfahan, dashed up the steps, rushed to the podium, and began, 'My noble lord and sire...'; but simultaneously with his words, Haladin began saying, 'Rashin, face the Sultan and state...'. Both men stopped, then started speaking again in unison, then stopped again. Rashin, despite his predicament, was visibly annoyed at being interrupted, while Haladin almost laughed in spite of himself. The minister glanced down at Jahid-Al-Rajahn; he too seemed amused. Finally Haladin said, 'Silence, Rashin! You will wait for my address to you as all others before you have waited.' He then pronounced the same formal instructions and then gave Rashin permission to speak.

"Rashin's contorted features and unruly hair and beard made him look more defiant than afraid. Yet, having long been accustomed to dissembling speeches, his voice was rich and attractive, and he now addressed the Sultan in the honey-toned manner of a nobleman: 'May the angels of heaven and the great powers of nature ever preserve the glorious reign of my noble sovereign, Sultan Jahid-Al-Rajahn. Sire, I consider it an opportunity—nay, an astonishing and undeserved privilege—to be able to speak directly to you, you who are the wisest of men and the most understanding of monarchs. Long have you known me to be one of your most faithful and attentive citizens.' Here there was a brief uproar from the crowd; Haladin raised his hand. 'Thank you, good Minister. Yes, Sire, long have you known of the devoutness of my citizenship and of my prowess as a combatant, which has done your majesty so much good service in the past. Now, while it is true that I have occasionally found myself embroiled in unfortunate quarrels with my fellow subjects, quarrels that were the wayward result of a heated brain and an undisciplined passion, I nonetheless feel these mishaps to be no more nor less than the accidental result of misdirected energy; energy, my lord, that I most fervently would wish to apply exclusively to your services. Therefore, with all due respect for the precise letter of the law of our land, and all praise to Allah, who sees and knows the maneuvers of every whim and fancy in our hearts, I wish to beg the following sentence from your Majesty: That I, Rashin of Tarakin, son of Kapur, be enlisted as a member of the Royal Guard to defend your highness's royal person, to aid the enforcement of the law of the land in all its particulars, and to combat all foreign enemies who encroach upon our free and fertile soil. In this way

I feel that I may both atone for my past crimes as well as do your Majesty the greatest of services.'

"The crowd went mad. People rose to their feet, screaming and shouting and shaking their fists at the criminal on the podium. Pieces of wood and stone came flying at Rashin from all directions. Still other people merely laughed and leaned against one another in jest. After a few minutes of this confused uproar, Haladin fiercely clapped his hands and commanded silence once again.

"The Sultan was undoubtedly surprised. He sat full back in his throne staring at Rashin with a perplexed expression that seemed to indicate both mirth and sorrow. But when he finally spoke, his voice was even and the words all too familiar, 'So be it.'

"The people were stunned. It was true that perhaps the time had come for the Sultan to begin showing a little mercy and understanding toward the common man and the unfortunate situations that poverty sometimes forces people into—but to allow an obvious criminal like Rashin not only to go free, but to serve in the Royal Guard! This was a 'Wisdom' that no one could, or would, comprehend.

"It is important for the reader to understand as well how unusual were all of the happenings of that fateful summer day. Never before had such reputable and disreputable people been tried; never before had a prisoner so much as turned his head unobtrusively, much less wailed in horror, rushed to the podium out of turn, or tried to escape; and never before had the Sultan betrayed any hint of mercy. Thus the tension among the on-lookers this day was so great that it defies description. Haladin himself was rather unnerved and began to feel the strain of keeping order during the proceedings. Only the Sultan seemed unconcerned, which did not make Haladin or the people any less uncomfortable.

"Still more unusual events were to follow. For now the first of the blond strangers, the taller man, ascended the platform and faced Jahid-Al-Rajahn. His aspect was proud, but no longer ar-rogant. There was even an air of humility about him when he spoke. In a clear even voice, he delivered the following speech, a speech that was remembered in Persia many years thereafter:

"'Jahid-Al-Rajahn, it is obvious by your demeanor and the respect you command from all your subjects that you are indeed a monarch worthy of the highest esteem. This is not the first time that I have had the privilege of addressing a great ruler; there-fore, I can say in all sincerity that no one deserves more in the way of honest words and just actions than yourself. It is true that I, Johann Hanauer, was attempting to avoid duty on a number of articles I had brought back from my travels in India. It is also true that I would not have hesitated, if the opportunity had presented itself, to bribe the necessary officials to pass through the land of Persia with so many more coins jingling happily in my purse. Nonetheless, I stand here before you now, my actions, although being reasonable—and to me fully justified—for the purposes of my business and my safe journey home, unfortunately running contrary to the current laws of your great kingdom. In my own defense, my great Lord, I can only say the following: The laws of any government are undoubtedly meant to be observed, and certainly enforced, at all times. However, what is a law if it be not the attempt of a civilized society to act in accordance with the great laws of nature and of God, laws that speak not only to the general good, but more importantly, to the individual conscience of every living being? And furthermore, what is the lasting good for any one of us, if we follow every law of society to the letter, yet learn not the lesson of following the dictates of our own heart and mind? For we all can see how easy it is to bear the appearance of civil decency in the bustle of the marketplace, yet abandon ourselves to every vice and caprice in the silence of our bosom. Is this what God wishes? Is this what we wish for ourselves? Unless a man learns to perceive what is true and just in each moment, and then acts in accordance with that perception, unless a man learns this, then I say he is no man. And this ability to see and act must be above all in accordance with the laws of God, even though the result may sometimes appear to oppose the specific dictates of a civilized people. It is from this point of view then that I extend to Sultan Jahid-Al-Rajahn my sincerest apologies for violation of your country's regulations and ask, because of the lack of any intended wickedness or avarice on my part, that I be given a full pardon and receive permission to continue on my journey homeward when this day's proceedings have ended.'

"When anyone, no matter how simple or sophisticated, experiences a series of unexpected turns of fortune in rapid succession, the result almost always serves to render the person at least momentarily silent to the whims of the present hour. And so it happened that the crowd on this hot summer afternoon did not react at all after this surprising and uplifting speech. Instead, not a few citizens turned their attention to the Sultan and awaited his reply. It was obvious that the Sultan had listened to Hanauers's speech very carefully. He watched calmly while he spoke and toward the end even began to smile as though he were actually happy. However, when the prisoner had finished, the Sultan frowned, leaned forward in his chair and whispered something to Haladin. Haladin then addressed Hanauer: 'The Sultan wishes to know on which objects you were so anxious to avoid paying duty.' The man replied, 'All of the gold jewelry, the two large stone friezes, and some women's garments.' The Sultan whispered to Haladin again. Haladin answered him, and the Sultan nodded. Then Jahid-Al-Rajahn rose and, still with a serious expression, said, 'So be it.'

"Hanauer smiled. 'Thank you, my lord. May you live long and happy.' As he descended the platform, his companion, who was noticeably delighted at the result, smiled in derision at Askfahan and then gazed admiringly at Hanauer. But the man did not meet his friend's gaze, and he was quietly escorted out of the arena.

"Now the final prisoner went up to the podium. Unlike every other afternoon in this Coliseum of Justice, the people now expected not another scourging, not another beheading, but yet another pardon. The shrewdness of the man's expression indicated that he felt the same way. He leaned casually against the railing and spoke to the Sultan as follows: 'Well, your Highness, it is obvious without doubt that you are a great man of wisdom. Even the sages of India do not compare with your incomparable breadth of vision. There is little more in the way of distinguished words that I can add to the noble speech of my great friend. Let me then be brief: I, Karl Hanson, am guilty of the same misdemeanor of avoiding duty on certain articles of valuable merchandise. I also would gladly have attempted to bribe my way through all opposition. Instead I could now, if you are willing'—and here he gestured to the Sultan—'receive a full pardon and continue homeward with my friend; or then again, I could serve, let us say, two years in your prison, if this will satisfy the dictates of your imperial decree. What do you say?'

"He looked at Jahid-Al-Rajahn and smiled. The Sultan smiled back, but did not speak right away. He whispered again to Haladin, and the minister said to Hanson, 'Pardon me, sir, but the Sultan is slightly confused. Which sentence are you suggesting for yourself, freedom or imprisonment?' Hanson shrugged, 'Imprisonment, if the Sultan agrees.' Abruptly the Sultan replied, 'So be it.'

"But now the man was horrified. His expression changed completely. He stared wildly at Jahid-Al-Rajahn, gripped the wooden railing, and screamed at the top of his voice, 'No! No! You give it to me! You vain pig!' The guard quickly rushed up the stairs and threw his hand over the prisoner's mouth. The man continued kicking and thrashing as he was dragged off the platform and thrown into the prisoner's chamber with the others.

Haladin rose and read the closing remarks for the day, and ended with the words, 'And let all men know that the sentence of Sultan Jahid-Al-Rajahn is still absolute dictator of justice in Tarakin….'"

That is all of the pertinent text. Binet goes on to present an analysis of the probable causes for the Royal Guard's growing dissatisfaction with the Sultan and a description of the attempted coup led by Askfahan. This need not concern us here, although it is interesting to note that Rashin remained loyal to Jahid-Al-Rajahn right to the end and even tried to warn him about Askfahan's plans. But fate decided otherwise. Anyway, in order to keep the flow of this particular tale intact, I will jump ahead and insert an extract from Haladin's journal. This entry is dated the morning after the unusual trial already described. It runs thus:

"It was not possible to sleep, not after such awesome events. My heart is still alive with every moment of it. I must write it all down before the freshness of it escapes me. Only five men came to trial yesterday…

"…But that evening I knew. The Sultan invited me to dine with him in private. It was clear that he was aware how much I felt the stress of the proceedings, and I was inwardly grateful to him for his generosity. Yet I was still in doubt as to the wisdom of his decisions. He must have guessed this as well for, after dinner, as we sat in silence on his balcony sipping tea and gazing out over the rooftops and minarets of Tarakin that were reddening in the warm evening glow of sunset, he began the following conversation:

"'Tell me, Haladin, is forgiveness necessary?'

"He broke the silence with this question without looking at me. I was startled, but answered at once. 'Yes my lord, when it is appropriate.'

"'And when is it appropriate?'

"'When a man is deserving of it.'

"'Can you say what it is that makes a man so deserving?'

"'Well,' I said, 'I suppose if he were really innocent, that speaks for itself. If he were not, then his own attitude and his circumstances must be taken into account as well.'

"He smiled at me and leaned forward in his chair. 'Which would you say is the more difficult action: To forgive yourself for a wrong you have committed or to forgive another man for wronging you?'

"'To forgive another man.'

"'Why?'

"The suddenness of this strange question all but silenced me. Finally I said, 'I am confused, my lord, as to your meaning. Surely the reasons are obvious.'

"The Sultan leaned back and sighed. He drank the rest of his tea and placed the cup on its saucer upside down. Then he looked at me so directly that it was rather unsettling. I noticed for the first time how sorrowful his expression was. It was not the sadness of a defeated man, but of one who knew perhaps more than he should. At last he spoke. 'I must explain something to you, Haladin, something I have never directly explained to anyone, although I have left indications of it for all to see. Today's trial makes it possible for me to speak freely. You will recall the tragic day when my son was killed during the boar hunt? At the time I was obsessed with the idea of his becoming a great hunter and soldier. I had, for example, spent many hours teaching him to hurl the lance. Late that afternoon we encountered an animal in the open field. Most of the party gave chase, but I held my son back and demanded that he take one practice throw at a tree before pursuing the boar itself. My anger made him nervous; he threw clumsily and missed. The anger welled black in my heart. I lashed out at him with my fist and struck him so hard that he fell senseless to the ground and broke his neck. He was killed instantly.'

" 'My lord, how...'

" 'Yes, Haladin, let me finish your question my own way: How could I forgive myself? Imagine my anguish! I let out a cry at once and, when everyone returned, gave the story of his horse rearing suddenly. No one suspected, everyone sympathized, but none of that could allay the feeling of horror at what I had done. When I locked myself inside my bed chamber that evening, I never expected to emerge again. I flung myself on the floor and wept more fiercely than I ever imagined possible. I had resolved that as soon as I had wrung every hot tear out of my breast, I would take my own life as the only possible retribution. Again and again that moment of senseless anger played itself out in my mind. Again and again I cursed my rashness, my callous indifference to everything but the satisfaction of my own whims. And the Furies did not stop there. For gradually all the foulness of my life, all the unchecked moments of pride and anger, all the impatience with my wife and ministers, all the decisions made from selfishness, all of this and more passed before my tormented heart in the silent darkness of that room and showed me without compromise who and what I really was. Gradually even tears seemed futile and were mere pinpricks beside the fire that illuminated all my sins. At moments I felt this torture alone would be enough to destroy me. But as I lay there, and as these memories repeatedly leered at me and accused me, a curious thing began to take place. I began to see all of these moments of weakness as though they were the deeds of another man. And the more I watched them in this way, the more I understood why they happened at all and what it was in me that caused them. The fire continued to burn, but it ceased to burn in accusation. It simply showed me what was there. And as the first rays of sunlight filtered through the lattice the next morning, I understood something very simple, yet very profound.'

"'What was that, my lord?'

"'I understood, Haladin, that I was my own accuser, my own judge and executioner. At first this realization filled me with great joy, as it enabled me to release myself from the hell of my self-inflicted recriminations. Understand me now—the awareness of my deeds remained more clearly, more indelibly than ever. But the necessity to accuse myself again and again ceased. Yet this was not enough. For I quickly saw that, as it is thus with me, so is it also with each single man. We accuse, we rage, we commit slander against one another, but in every case it is not another, but ourselves whom we are debasing. And now a new sense of guilt began to well up inside of me. For I could not but think of that monstrosity of "justice" that I had created in the form of my arena. Such stupidity! To place my own sentence on the heads of other men! For the rest of that day and most of the next, I thought and thought as to how I might rid myself of this artificial horror. Simply to free everyone would have been of no use. The populace might have started to settle matters in their own way with suspected criminals. So how to proceed, what to do? And then—then the answer came to me, again quite simply and clearly; and the rest, more or less, you know. From that day forward, I resolved to pass no sentence on any man, but let each person look to that himself.'

"So he finished his remarkable story and grew silent again. But I did not sufficiently ponder what he had said and felt obliged to call him to account. 'But forgive me, sire—how can you say that you ceased passing sentence on our prisoners? After your decree was issued and after you began coming to the arena, the beatings and executions continued as before.'

"'Each man chose his own end.'

"'But they were not aware of other alternatives! You did not specify.'

"'What is that to me, Haladin? But, yes, you are right. Truly I was naïve as to how men treat themselves! After the first two afternoons in the arena, I realized how almost impossible it is for

a man to forgive himself. People simply do not see this as a possibility; and even when they do, to act on it takes more strength
than most are capable of. You see, Haladin, it would have been
to no advantage for me to indicate this. If I did so, perhaps more
of these men, dishonest or otherwise, would still be walking
through the marketplace today, but they themselves would be
exactly the same. No, it is a decision that each must come to
himself, or not at all.'

"'And do you think today it happened? Rashin...'

"'Yes, yes, it did. I must tell you that the continual spectacle
of men foolishly ending or ruining their lives for no reason began
to weigh heavily on me. This afternoon, as I entered the arena,
I began to feel that my whole scheme was nothing more than a
fiendish joke that Allah had placed in my mind to torment me
further for the death of my son. The judgments of Percleon and
Aziz seemed to confirm this.'

"'Was not Percleon's action noble?'

"'Was it? It seems so difficult to follow a friend into death.
Yet is it not more difficult, more heroic, to stand by the most precious thing that a man possesses and go on living? No, Percleon's
deed was no less automatic than all who had preceded him.'

"'But now, Rashin...'

"'Ha! Yes, Rashin! He is a rascal, is he not? Of course, he
may have been lying to me. Yet if he wants to think that I was
deceived by his speech, that is his affair. In all likelihood, he
has not forgiven himself—but he probably never accused himself
either! But my decision still applies. People like Rashin are their

own punishment; no matter if they go on living and continue with their knavery, they still must live with themselves. We will watch Rashin—he will not be allowed to speak with me. So have no fear.'

"'Were you happy when the European merchant spoke so nobly?'

"'Beyond words, Haladin. It was necessary to conceal my joy from the people by asking those questions about the merchandise. Since his decision was also his own, I could not too readily reveal to everyone my secret. But how he spoke! Every word described my feeling exactly! Would that all of us could live this way at all times. I made a rough copy of his speech. Our scribes will preserve it for our offspring.'

"The Sultan's noble mood made me feel warm and free inside. But there was still one more question. 'And the merchant's companion, sire? Could you not just free him as well?'

"Jahid-Al-Rajahn became momentarily sad. 'This is just what he wanted. Unlike his friend, who spoke sincerely, this other man was clever enough to guess the meaning of my "sentencing." But like many men who learn something that it is better not to learn, his vanity overpowered him, and he expected me to relent and to grant him his pardon myself. Such a fool! Of course, if he had chosen freedom, he would have been no better off than Rashin. So it matters not.'

"I hesitated, 'Still, he did know the truth. His challenge probably came more from humor than from malice.'

"'That may be true, Haladin, but they were his own words.'

"'And will you make him serve the entire two year sentence?'

"'Every hour.'

"By now dusk had settled heavily over the whole city. We both sat again for several minutes without speaking. Through the tranquil silence of the darkness and warm evening air there arose the solitary cry of the muezzin with his final call to prayer. I thought of the people of Tarakin then, of how each man and woman will hear these plaintive tones and respond to them in a different way: Some will kneel and pray fervently; some will pause momentarily over their food or conversation; some will fall into slumber; some will wait peevishly until it is no more; perhaps many will hardly hear it at all. Yes, each will embrace it in his own way. Just as we embrace, or reject, everything that comes to us through our life. This indeed is the sentence, the only sentence, that Jahid-Al-Rajahn so profoundly illustrates for all of us. A man sees what he wants to see, hears what he wants to hear, is what he wants to be. And whether we will or will not embrace what almighty Allah sends our way is dependent on our own choosing. Oh, may the great powers on high ever grant me the discretion to know and do what is right and just, and may they ever preserve the sacred wisdom of our noble sovereign, and my esteemed lord, Jahid-Al-Rajahn. So be it.'"

This is the end of Haladin's entry. A fascinating conclusion to an equally fascinating beginning. It does seem to me unfair after reading these events to consider what an unhappy end awaited

Haladin and the Sultan. Binet gives numerous details (including a few gory ones, as you might expect), but in short it went like this: Askfahan's strategy on the evening of 3 May, 12__ was to seal off the gates of Tarakin, then one by one seize all the male officials and royalty of the palace in their sleep and send them off bound and gagged out of the city and into the neighboring mountains. Although he wanted power and considered himself a more competent administrator than the Sultan, Askfahan was by no means ruthless and hoped to avoid bloodshed at all costs. He also thought that in this way he could more quickly win the support of the general public. But after about two hours of successful maneuvers, there came of a sudden a tremendous scream and uproar from the top floor of the palace. Torches were lit, men shouted, several villagers poured out into the streets. Askfahan and a band of followers stole away into the labyrinth of roads and alleys, hoping to conceal themselves in the cloak of darkness until the confusion passed. But two young boys followed them and called after the loyal members of the Guard, who quickly gave chase.

What had happened was that two of Askfahan's soldiers could not resist the sight of the beautiful Tayana, Haladin's daughter, sleeping peacefully without any garments or blankets. They immediately lost their senses and somehow concluded that they could enjoy her quietly without any fuss and then continue on their mission. Of course, the exact opposite of what they expected happened, and soon Haladin and the Sultan himself were upon them. Unfortunately the would-be kidnappers were far better swordsmen, and before long both of these great men were lying in their own royal blood. Tayana was killed as well before the guards could finally put an end to the intruders. About two hours afterward, Askfahan and his men were surrounded. Rashin was among the foremost of the pursuers, and he stood forward with tears in his eyes and cried, "Know, Askfahan that your treachery has led to the death of the noblest man who ever governed a people! Now stand forth and prepare to taste the vengeance of my hot steel." Askfahan went white. He stood frozen for a few moments, his lips trembling, and said finally, "The death of Jahid-Al-Rajahn was never my intention or desire. But since I alone am responsible for it, then you must know, Rashin, that there is only one thing for me to do."

And with that, he fell on his sword.

THE END

The Pigeon and the Squirrel

The Pigeon and the Squirrel

THERE WAS ONCE an elderly gentleman who, after his retirement, took the greatest pleasure in visiting the local city park every afternoon. In fact, there probably were, and are, many such gentlemen, but this story concerns only one of them. His name could have been Rowles, or Corbey, or maybe even Stark. For the sake of convenience, though, we can pretty safely assume that we do not know his name. Nor do we know which city—and by extension which park in that city—it was. In the wintertime, he would wear a long plaid coat that buttoned right up from his knees all the way to his Adam's apple. It, in fact, nearly covered this symbolic remnant of our forebears' first sin, and an olive green scarf neatly finished off the concealment. The two deep pockets of the coat were of the greatest service to the gentleman, not solely because of his stubborn refusal to wear gloves, but far more significantly because they afforded a practical means of conveying the nearly two pounds of nuts, raisins and cracker bits that always accompanied him on his daily sojourn. These provisions were cleverly arranged in layers in two clear plastic bags, and the bags were then slipped down into the big pockets. This way everything remained clean, orderly and well-hidden. The man greatly disliked having to turn his pockets inside out every evening and shake off food remnants into the waste bin. Luckily his invention made it unnecessary for him to do this, because even the mere thought of it made him cringe. Now since these foods were arranged in layers, he could consistently surprise both himself and those he fed by what would come out of his pockets next. First it was a handful of broken-up pretzels, then a few salted peanuts, then raisins and coconuts, walnut meats, cheese crackers, jelly beans, more peanuts, and still more pretzels. On about every fifth handful, the man sometimes popped one or two morsels into his own mouth, while all the rest was liberally dispersed along the paved walkways and little plots of green. Usually, though, he contented himself with licking the salt off his fingers.

As he slowly made his way around the park, he was, as one could readily imagine, accompanied by a horde of hungry urban fauna. The most notable species were, again as everyone can easily picture to him or herself, the grey pigeon and the equally grey squirrel. A few sparrows could manage to steal in among the bigger birds now and then and nip away with a few stray pieces. But usually size would win out over stealth in this particular phenomenon of nature, and so the little ones never, for example, managed to get hold of a jelly bean. Of course the sparrows would say that they did not like jelly beans anyway. And, whether or not this was indeed the sincere statement of an essential preference, the attitude they voiced well harmonized with the facts of the situation.

The benefactor of these perpetually ravenous creatures had an uncanny ability to recognize individuality amidst a sea of darting beaks and bushy tails. He would often call to one or another of them by name and coax them forward with a fat cashew or walnut. "Priscilla, I saved this one just for you. Max—look what I have here, Max. Oscar, now let Max take it, and I'll give you the next." On one particular occasion (to which this story refers)—although actually it was on most occasions—Oscar was not so obedient, and in a moment, nut in mouth, he loped across the grass and scurried up the gnarled hump of a tall oak. Max was not upset about this. Amid so much plenty, a little impudence could be tolerated. The man rewarded his patience by placing a large sugary raisin on his left shoulder and bending down slightly, "Here you go, Max boy." The squirrel responded at once and leapt up with one quick spring. He sat there on his haunches and licked and nibbled in his nervous way. He decided to go at it slowly and thereby savor not only the sweet morsel in his claws but also the unusual perspective he now enjoyed. Below him his friends of fur and of feather continued to move freely in and among each other. The pigeons maintained a steady chorus of coos, which the squirrel knew to be burping, while his own breed kept dashing away to hide their prizes and then returning again for more, with all that practicality peculiar to a warm-blooded species. The squirrel then eyed the back of the man's neck, which revealed a profusion of black and grey hairs. Deciding it would be a good idea to thank the man for his gift, he leaned forward and gave a gentle tug on the neck with his teeth. The skin seemed to ripple appreciatively, which made the squirrel extra happy.

Now it could have been by chance or it could have been by design that a choice remnant of cheese cracker happened to land on the shoulder opposite from the one the squirrel was perched upon. In either case it definitely was there. The creature started up nervously and twitched his nose. When he was sure that all was safe, he began considering whether or not to hop across after the savory bit and so offset the taste of sweetness in his mouth. Suddenly there was a rustle of air above him, like that of someone shaking out a wet cloth, and the next moment a huge grey pigeon alighted on the other shoulder. The newcomer bobbed his head up and down a few times, aimed an inquisitive eye at his rival and snatched up the cracker bit with one flick of beak and gullet. The squirrel was a little disappointed, but he went back to his raisin without making a comment.

"Do you believe in free will?" the pigeon asked.

"Never thought of it as something to believe in," the squirrel replied. "These theories often seem like imposition to me. You reach down, you pick up a cracker, you eat it. Then after the fact we wonder about whether we willed it to happen or whether we merely responded to a familiar stimulus."

"We respond to unfamiliar stimuli as well," the pigeon pointed out. The squirrel agreed with this remark so readily that the bird realized it was unnecessary to elaborate. He went on, "Yet if we could establish that responding to stimuli was a first principle, an *a priori* fact of life, this would not by definition exclude the possibility of free will. We would simply have to consider will—or more precisely, the volition of the personal subject—on an entirely different basis. That is to say the phenomenon of stimulus-response is given; we accept that. And therefore many actions that we formerly ascribed to personal decision, such as eating, flying, excreting…"

"Please, sir, not while we are having lunch. It is a terrible habit of your species. Just because you have wings does not give you all the privilege of disregarding certain social courtesies. No wonder this race here call you 'foul.' "

"Not quite, sir. That is mere coincidence. But I will respect your request and demonstrate to you mammals that continence is a habit not all that difficult of attainment. Let me not, however, stray too far from my line of thought. We have seen how much of our behavior is driven; it is not decided. Therefore, what would the true nature of free will be? Or no, let me ask the question like this: Under what circumstances do we make a choice and act upon that choice entirely from within ourselves?"

"That is quite enough, you know. If we act upon our choice and do not succeed, can we call the action will? Must there not be some tangible result? Must there not be a ripple on the pond that we can call our own?" The pigeon began to open his beak, but the squirrel stopped him. "I am afraid, sir, that I must ask you, before we go any further, to back up just a little bit. For I am not entirely convinced that our behavior is 'driven' as you say. Can you demonstrate more clearly what you mean?"

"I can, but I must appeal to the poet in you. For it is only through an inspired analysis of everyday impressions that we can push beyond our ordinary modes of thought. Now look, here we have a wonderful example arriving just at the right moment."

So saying the pigeon immediately plunged his beak into the mound of delicious tidbits that the spread fingers of one hand had just elevated up to collarbone level. The squirrel bit hard into his raisin to keep from laughing out loud at this obvious lack of self-control. The bird pecked about at lightning speed to gather in as much as possible before the hand descended. It did, and reappeared at the feet of the squirrel. Intent upon demon-strating his own capacity for restraint, the little mammal kept his claws to his breast and cast one eye, and then the other, down at the delectable pile. He turned his head back and forth several times, the deliberateness of his scrutiny pleasing himself almost as much as his lunch. Having scouted out the location of the three biggest nuts, he waited until the mound began to descend and, with three quick snatches, had them at his feet.

A silence ensued, broken only by a few occasional coos from the bird. "I beg your pardon," he said and turned half around. The squirrel did his best to restrain his feelings of pride. He picked up a smooth pecan and looked it over with mock admiration, while the heart in his breast pounded away like a corn kernel popping and re-popping. Unable to restrain himself after three or four minutes, he said in as even a tone as he could manage, "It is rather difficult to resist, this stimulus-response business."

The pigeon looked a bit doleful. "I admire your ability to grasp the—if you will—kernel of the problem so quickly." The squirrel suppressed a grin. The bird went on, "One moment the process of speaking gives us each the illusion of an active subject; the next moment our heads are literally turned by an all-too-familiar stimulus." The squirrel considered "our heads" an amusing attempt at democratizing the situation and could not help but say, "So it becomes a matter of employing techniques similar to the ones I used to begin to wriggle off this Skinnerian hook?"

The pigeon did not flinch at the reference. He was a trifle too confused for that. "Oh?" he queried and cocked an eye at his companion. "What technique was that?"

"Well, you saw it, old man. Just offer a little resistance. We all can do it if we remember soon enough."

"Humph," the pigeon said and looked around. "Humph," he said a second time. He took a moment to pick at his breast and neck and then turned full-eye again on the squirrel. "Sorry to say this, my friend, but surely you must have realized by now that there are responses and there are responses. I agree that my own impetuosity sets me flying off in any direction sooner than I would like, but the circumspect behavior of your own species is no less predictable, though it does present a more sober appearance, for which I do sometimes envy you. But at that, covetousness is just another response. It all is. There was a…"

The bird wanted to continue, but he saw how embarrassed the squirrel had become. He lowered his voice and said in a soothing tone, "Don't take it so hard now, friend. I am sure there is a way out of this. That is why I raised the subject with you in the first place."

"Is friendship just another response?" the squirrel said bitterly. He straightened himself up and looked at the black and grey hairs that stood just a few hairs away. "But you know… oh sorry, what is your name?"

"Steadley. And yours?"

"Trentorius. Yes, it is curious that. My name, I mean. This man here has delighted in referring to me by some kind of monosyllabic utterance. I don't know what I've done to deserve only one syllable, while my brother Pandarikan gets two. Perhaps the man considers him cleverer than myself because he is always snatching at my food with all the bumptiousness of a pi…"— Trentorius cleared his throat—"…of a polar bear."

"Never met one of those," Steadley said dryly.

"Now it is all so rudely obvious. A spray of food rattles on the ground. I hear it, see what I am most familiar with, and gobble it up. The man is attracted to my movements. He watches me eat. I watch him, ready for the next mouthful or ready to run off if he turns out to be like some of the other imbeciles around here. He sees me stare and takes it for affection. He comes closer. I stiffen up. He gets happy and smiles. His lips open out and the voice emits 'Max.' If I could emit the way he does, I would probably come back with 'Kangfinkle' or 'Snashmagibber.' Then he puts a succulent raisin drop on his shoulder. Who can resist? So here I am, filling my gut as usual, and it is only by accident that the location of the raisin now has me about five-and-a-half feet off the ground. Oh gods, it is all ridiculous. So now we talk about this. So what? Tonight Pandarikan and I will talk about the ladies. Or we'll fight. Oh gods, gods, it is all nothing. Wind and leaves. We're just wind and leaves." Trentorius' face darkened. He even dropped the pecan he was holding and made no effort to stop it from falling to the ground.

"I have never been partial to existential colorings," Steadley consoled him. "I have had my unhappy moments vis-a-vis these reflections, as you are having now. What I only just discovered today, though, was a wonderous application of the principle 'to embrace the leper.' In other words, instead of treating our pre-dicament as abhorrent, treat it as though things could not, and should not, be otherwise. And therein lies the m-m-m-m-mir-mira-the miracle!" He shouted out this last word and flapped off into the cold air. Trentorius watched him make two wide circles above the trees and jettison a few grey and white dribbles. In a minute he realighted and preened himself all over.

"Oh, ooh, ahhh, oh. So that is what is called 'going to the toilet,' eh? More difficult than I thought. Anyway, I swore to master this new habit, and master it I shall."

On any other day, Trentorius would have enjoyed quite a laugh over this. But his depression did not leave him, and he went on to point out, "You cannot tell me that this way lies free-dom. So you acquire a new habit. That is just a rearrangement of stimuli. Your bowels begin telling you to fly off into seclusion rather than to air raid the nearest head or building. I see no mastery of self here. Little human children learn it without even knowing it."

"Oh, my dear man! You have hit upon it! That is the whole point—'without our knowing it.' Do you not see?"

The squirrel grumbled that indeed he did see, although he admitted he did not exactly see what Steadley was trying to say just now.

"It has to do with a perception that came to me this morning. And let me start by reiterating the truth of this important fact, namely, that perceptions come to us, we do not go out and apprehend them ourselves. Even the theories surrounding stimulus-response—including the attempts to demonstrate it empirically and to elaborate upon it philosophically—come into the mind without provocation. Our minds react in one way or another to the energy of ideas, just as our lungs and nostrils respond to a rush of fresh December air: we take in what we can and savor what we can, and then it passes. And somehow we know that there is always more of it than any one of us can hold.

"With that in mind consider how it was with me when I awoke today. I had spent the night on the ledge of a municipal building, rather high up, nestled between two elaborate granite carvings. When I opened my eyes, the sky was grey and overcast, and a light rain was falling everywhere. The air was cold and I shivered at once. Fortunately the overhang kept me dry. Perhaps because I was still dozing a bit and enjoying the luxuriance of a slow wakefulness, I was unusually passive to the many impressions of morning city life entering into me. The dampness kept prodding at my sleepiness; the sweet drone of my companions along the ledge stirred my heart toward the wish for talk and amusement; the sound of car horns in the depths below reminded me of the daily responsibility of feeding; and my knotted stomach began to remind me of the same. Just then a flock of my friends fluttered out and down toward the street corner. I watched them turn and fall in large circles that became smaller and more focused as they narrowed toward a waste bin next to the traffic light. The image of them all descending thus reminded me of a benign tornado. My stomach and the reflex of my legs could not resist. I leapt out into the wet air. Drops pattered against my neck and chest. I fell heavy into space and opened myself out. A soft rush of wind hit me from below; the air billowed around me and made me shudder. I then sailed easily into the queue and wheeled to the street. The sounds increased—car horns, bus horns, truck horns, skidding rubber, a herd of footsteps, shouts, chatter. The meal was wonderful, a cluster of sweet pistachios. Boots and shoes were prolific, and I got very wet. I ate as fast as possible and thrust myself back up to the ledge. I found my same spot and shook myself out. Below the river of iron and of flesh continued, the rain fell, my friends went straggling off around the buildings for morning sport. I tried to settle back into my former state of repose and regarded the wall of cloud above.

"How can it be explained? Everything was the same, and yet different. I know not the cause. But can you not see, Trentorius, the miracle of it all unfolding? The movement of life, and I—and you—a part of it? The million, million wheels and levers turning, the lovely interplay of energies, the rushing air and its buoyant curve around my wing and body, the discarded nuts that fed a necessity where none seemed to exist, the wooden arms that shelter your own brood, your nails that can so neatly fix themselves into its bark, this perch we have now adopted that feeds us both with candy and fortuitous talk. Of course, things penetrate and animate each other! Of course! The real secret here is not to defend the begrudging subject, the voice in us who would insist on 'decision' or 'choice.' My proud wings say, 'I ride the wind,' yet the wind may well be saying, 'I bear aloft and push where I do wish this pompous scavenger.' And yet it is not so on either side. We without knowing it are now response and now another's stimulus. And nowhere in it all can we say 'I.' What seems so individual to crow or to man is often proved the merest froth."

Trentorius remembered the easy way his own self-love was stirred one moment back and could not but concede the point. The concession, however, made his gloom more firm. "Granted that if we learn to accept this, Steadley, and to even revel in this sea of uncaused and unmotivated action, our pleasure and our understanding remain circumscribed. So now we witness the cosmic fishbowl. The goldfish, by not mentally willing his gills to do what they already do so well, has simply killed off a sentiment, one which I am not entirely convinced was to his or anyone else's detriment. We remain in prison."

Both creatures paused for refreshment as the palm-borne mound returned. The squirrel gave the neck another tug of appreciation, and the pigeon imitated this with a few gentle pecks of his own. The skin squirmed with delight and approval.

"You see, Steadley, how it is? This sort of thing goes by the name of 'affection' or 'friendship' or 'love.' We need not give such names to manifestations like this. The connotation is all wrong."

"So to what should such connotations apply! And where do the connotations of love and friendship come from anyway? No, no, Trentorius, you are letting the argument sweep you away into one-dimensional answers. Surely this new unhappiness of yours is just another shade of vanity. Let it pass, man, let it pass. It is not real."

This appeal to the heart flustered the stubborn squirrel. He accidently kicked away another nut and for a moment contemplated leaping after it. When he righted himself and saw the pigeon's eye upon him again, he clenched his teeth for a moment and then spluttered into a loud laughing fit. The pigeon's head and throat began to throb vigorously as he laughed along in his own way.

"You have me tamed," the squirrel said finally, "Lead on."

"Nowhere but to here," Steadley replied after catching his breath. "It is curious to observe how all speculation, no matter how critical, how abstract or how casuistic, leads back inevitably to an appeal to our highest understanding of the lived moment. Yet living that moment remains the essential responsibility, and it is everyone's concern. Not philosophers alone need to look through their own eyes and their own hearts. As we know,

philosophers often make a muddle of it. If we take our conclusion about stimulus-response—or 'interdependency,' as I would
now prefer to call it—we find not another gilding of the cage
but rather a renewed and vigorous affirmation of our mutual
responsibilities as living beings. We know how between lovers
and friends the slightest glance or change in intonation of the
voice can rouse the greatest tremors in each other. The same
is true to varying degrees between everyone and everyone else.
The clothes and trinkets people wear, the attitude of posture and
walk, the very thoughts we enrobe in the closets of our brain, all
of this emits from us and interpenetrates the lives and minds of
nature, root and branch. It is naïve to underestimate the extent
of this penetration. There are certain pens whose work continues
to reverberate through centuries, and who can doubt but that the
simplest gesture of kindness toward someone a little tired or a
little distracted can reverberate just as solemnly."

The squirrel rose up to his full height, and at this point in
the pigeon's discourse rushed in with inspired words of his own
to sustain the poetry of their converse.

"Friendship is conscious acknowledgment of Nature's inter-
dependent members. The hand I hold or the ear that attends to
my word is as necessary to the soul as my own wayward tongue.
The deeper the gesture to a friend is recognized, the more elec-
tric our communion with the world. The highest friend is the
highest servant, he most removed from storing away an account
of good deeds to nibble through the winter of his loneliness.
Unhappy he who 'decides' to talk to someone, who 'chooses' to

lean on a necessary shoulder. What becomes paramount is this awareness and our appropriate response to it. For true awareness without true action is the death of deaths."

"Aagh," said the pigeon.

"No question, then, but that we are ruled from the top down. As in right order the head and not the loins condition proper conduct, so are the highest principles of love and truth the movers of the world and not the baubles of a mediocre wish. The mediocre win only baubles. To conform to the highest is to turn the hurricane of complacency against you. It is why the habit of forbearance yields more than the habit of indulgence, although a timely moment of indulgence may uproot a pretended mastery. So futile is it to codify right action or to quantify obedience to an angel; and yet, so obvious to each other are the pretenses we wear, and so obvious to ourselves what we do not—yet must—do."

"Aargh!"

"To marvel at the laws of Nature is a privilege. To begrudge those laws is itself one of the laws but one that we can be free from. The silver thread that guides us step-by-step through our day takes us past every niche of the labyrinth of our heart. Nothing is omitted. As we explore and comprehend each cul-de-sac, we can leave it behind with understanding. It is when we do not see a cul-de-sac as such that we continue to return there and confront the beast of our vanity, he the most lost of all. And here we arrive at the answer to our initial questions. The nature of free will is necessity—our necessity—that no one else can live for us. The choices can only be our own, and the right choice brings the right success, though success will often masquerade as its opposite. For what, in this world of ours, does not? Time is the revealer and the answerer, so to expect instantaneous conclusions is to sup upon one's own saliva."

"Aaahhhh!" Steadley hurried off into the topmost branches of the oak where Trentorius kept his home.

The squirrel watched him for a moment but then decided to use this pause in the conversation to glance around again. He turned about and looked out in the same direction as the gentleman. The open green and the walkways were deserted. One young couple huddled together on a bench. In the far distance the mesh of black tree branches seemed to implore an indifferent winter sky. Since they were at virtually the same eye level, Trentorius could not help but notice how little the scene must be changing for the man. The head did not turn, the eyes were fixed, and the figure moved forward at glacial speed. The chilly air grew moist and a fine drizzle soon enveloped them.

The pigeon arrived back after a few minutes. He puffed out his body and gave his feathers a hardy shake. The squirrel rinsed the nut remnants out from between his teeth and expectorated over the side.

"There remains," Trentorius said at last, "the question of pain."

"Exactly," Steadley affirmed. "And it is probably worth noting at once that there is no answer in the sense of an 'explanation.' One is inevitably forced either to yield to misery or to appeal to a higher understanding. Any claims to a midway solution, or to a refusal to acknowledge that suffering is a part of every life, result in stifled experiences and a topsy-turvey sense of pleasure and pain."

"Like presuming to enjoy moldy walnuts," Trentorius mused and fingered around his teeth again. "Yes, it is true what you say, Steadley. I recall a few years back a young woman who used to sit on a bench on the other side of the field there. It was springtime. She arrived about ten each morning with a book and a bottle of water. The book was usually a novel, and the water was usually bubbly and salty. She offered me a cupful on a few occasions, but I found the brew decidedly gruesome. The mid-morning light made her a glorious spectacle to behold. Her hair was yellow, and she would allow the gentle wind to toss strands of it across her face as she read. She kept such a serious posture while turning page after page, but this intellectual demeanor only made her full lips and swelling bosom look more delightful and more sweetly feminine. I tell you, my friend, many an hour I spent out on a limb because of this woman."

"I concluded as much," the pigeon remarked.

"This delicate beauty beguiled me for a long time. But eventually I saw the deeper truth of the matter. She always bristled, you know, when someone passed by who gave indications of wanting to stop and chat with her. At first this behavior pleased me, since it meant I could continue to have her all to myself. Then other things began to reveal themselves. There was the fact—perhaps obvious to yourself, since you know how humans are—that she was almost never reading. I watched several times how her eye wavered across the page for a few moments, only to pause, glaze over, and stare downward. When the clouds laid bare the sun or the breeze wafted some spring perfume under her nose, the body responded with obvious sighs of pleasure. But the sighs were heavy, and the pleasure in her frame was not carried through to her face, that is to say her heart. And soon the regularity of her visits disturbed me as well. Punctuality can indicate diligence or despair, the latter state of mind arising from the need to embrace a small detail, since there is no one else and no other purpose to embrace. No one is more on time around here than the vagabonds. Sorrow emulates the moon, both in its regular turnings and in the display of a reflected happiness that conceals unseen conflict. I so wished that I could have done something for her. By June she was gone forever. That is the way, is it not, Steadley? When one refuses to accept pain thoroughly into oneself and let it run its course, when one continues to imagine that it is just another day and everything is just fine, the sorrow cannot but linger. Then the worst of all happens—people get used to it and expect nothing else."

"It was a wise man who said that one needs to turn life on its head," Steadley continued. "The moments of suffering that come to us are actually the opportunity for a great leap forward. Let us suppose your beloved idol had lost a dear friend or had herself decided to separate from him. The result of such a rupture is a great release of energy. A thousand memories surge up again and again. The heart repeatedly asks why, the mind repeatedly searches for answers, and only wet eyes reply. This energy, this complete upheaval in a seemingly blissful existence, pushes one forward into new realms. Everything appears to be the same: our clothes, our living space, our daily routines, our interests. But now the opening of a letterbox in the morning, the smile at a fruit vendor on the street corner, the book one is reading with so much interest... somehow there is a shift. We realize how unimportant certain things are. This moment, though seemingly imperceptible, may be cataclysmic. One stands in a different relationship to the whole of life. Consider the passage of our solar system through the zodiac. Imperceptibly, yet with constant and irreversible force, the array of galaxies and worlds and suns is ever newly displaced. A universe recedes forever and a new one appears."

"It is interesting to observe your tendency now to use human life as the key example for this part of the discussion. And I wholly concur. I would just caution you, my friend, to perhaps not speak too intellectually about all of this. Your large-scale perspective is essential, and a wounded heart can benefit from a universal sense of scale, but let us not forget that what hurts, hurts. There remains something uncompromising, and seemingly unjust, about it all. The air you abide upon gives you an overview that no one on four legs can match. Yet distance has its shortcomings."

"I will agree with you immediately, Trentorius, so that we need not argue the point. I am reminded now of another remark you made a moment ago. 'Let sorrow run its course.' How true that is! Time and Change are the very stuff of the material world, much more so than atoms, neutrinos and all that other rubbish. If I split a split hair, it will just disappear quicker. There is nothing 'solid' about matter. There is nothing fixed about our bodies nor the lives they lead. The material world is one of flitting phantoms. It is higher understanding, basic love and spirit, that are the real solid stuff. Were we not in touch with such firmness, we would be gone with the next upward draught."

"Yes, and pain makes these higher realities still more solid. A heart seasoned by experience lets in so much more of common sense and decency."

"The only terminal victim of suffering is our self-esteem. Let it rail against injustice as it flies away."

"A sudden shock can change a life. Rightly taken, there is no longer the need to be safe. One discovers the peril behind a supposed assurance."

"Daily routines need distraction. The more smoothly a man rolls through his day, the more certain we can be that he is rolling downhill."

"Real living and real understanding require speed, lift, enthusiasm."

"Pain provides the fuel."

"The unexpected teaches respect for mystery."

"They who can rightly administer shocks must do so."

"They must."

The two friends grew silent at the same moment. Something was instantly communicated through this silence that begged immediate action. Both creatures drew themselves up to full height. There followed a brief hesitancy, as often happens when a mutual decision appears without words to celebrate it. Each cocked one full eye at the other, then turned the head and showed the other eye. They went back around like this one more time, and were both finally satisfied. Then the squirrel and the pigeon reared back their heads, opened their mouths as wide as possible, and struck full force into the unsuspecting neck that stood between them.

The young couple on the bench were mingling noses, cheeks and hot breath to keep the chill away from their intimacy. But this intimacy was at this moment shattered by a horrific blood-curdling shriek. Boy and girl started up and saw the old man, about fifty paces off, throwing his arms about wildly in the air and pouring forth an embarrassing off-color rondo, of which the phrase "filthy ungrateful bastards" served as principle theme. The pigeons flew up in unison like a reverse waterfall and billowed into a cloud that made a few easy turns around the field. The squirrels leapt into nearby branches in their shrewd and supple way and watched the man with anxious eyes. The poor fellow flung his two bags of food high in the air and let it all scatter on the grass. He half-trotted away toward the park gate in an awkward manner. As he went he pulled his coat pockets inside out and shook them with evident disgust.

The animals returned and feasted until dark. No one ever saw the man come to the park again. Perhaps he heard and eventually understood some of the dialogue that had taken place so close to his ears. Whispers of new learning often require delay for their import to filter down to our humdrum affairs. And it may be that if you or anyone else spent a few extra hours in a neighborhood park, the indigenous creatures might offer you some of their wisdom at the price of a cracker. Just do not expect to be able to force it from them. The squirrels would simply scurry up the trunk of a tree and flirt their tails at you, while the pigeons would waddle off and perhaps give a nervous flap of their wings, if they sensed that you were getting a little too close.

The Giver of Gifts

The Giver of Gifts

EVERY DAY ROLAND WAS HAPPY. In the morn-
ing he left his cottage with a kiss on both cheeks to his
plump little wife. Then off he would go into the town to
buy and sell his antiques and to make his beautiful jewelry. As he
opened the door of his shop, he smiled at the tinker next door;
and as he swept away the dust from the pavement, he waved to
the shopkeeper across the road. The people who walked past his
window each morning were always greeted with a similar glow
of delight when they saw that large round face glance up from
its work and smile at them merrily with the jeweler's lens stuck
in one eye. And needless to say, his customers were treated the
best of all. Many townspeople visited the shop each day just to
receive Roland's jasmine tea and cream cakes and to hear his
delightful stories, jokes, and anecdotes, all delivered with that
same energetic ebullience that seemed as indefatigable for him
to impart as it was wholly pleasurable for others to receive. Every
afternoon Roland would pause over his labor for a light meal of
bread and meat and a glass of beer. He would sit in front of his
shop on the red painted stool that he had made for himself when
a boy, and eat his lunch and talk to the passers-by. After lunch he
would sometimes tilt his stool back on two legs against the brick

wall and stare up at the sky for several minutes, and then return to his labor and his custom. And afterward, when the evening brought an end to his long and productive day of employment, Roland would return home again to his happy little family, feeling just as jolly and content as he had been the moment he had left them that same morning.

Twice a year Roland opened the doors of his shop to all and sundry and gave away whatever he possessed at the time to whoever wanted it. Porcelain teacups, platters and cake plates, framed etchings, lithographs and oils, brass chandeliers and silver candlesticks, inlaid tables, mahogany cabinets, leather armchairs, musical instruments, crystal vases, copper pots and pans, marble statues and plaster casts, sundials, tapestries, woven carpets, hand-made lace, jade figurines, glass bead and pearl necklaces, cameos, rings, bracelets, watches, cigarette holders, cuckoo clocks, peacock feathers, velvet pillowcases: all this and everything else that happened to be lying about the four corners of his bountiful establishment was offered up to the general populace every fifteenth of January and fifteenth of July. Nearly every citizen of the village would visit Roland's shop on these two days for at least a brief glance at what the happy man had on display, yet seldom would anyone remove one of his beautiful articles carelessly or just for the sake of taking it. Roland's generosity was so sincere and so ingenuous that it compelled others to be honest and open with him as well. So visitors basically only took what they truly needed or truly wanted, and both they themselves and the jolly proprietor remained perfectly content.

But such a sight it was on those "days of gift giving" as Roland himself called them! People poured out of the front door of the shop and into the street carrying mirrors, glassware, tea kettles, stuffed animals, or whatever else caught their fancy. Men and women laughed and chatted and showed each other their new possessions. Inside the shop Roland hurried from one patron to the next, handing out cookies and tea and explaining the value and usefulness of every article, from the grandest walnut and marble sideboard to the tiniest mother of pearl hatpin. The women discussed and compared articles for hours on end, while the children dashed about in between the aisles of furniture and clothing with a host of giggles and shouts. Whenever Roland tired of talking, he would sit at his workbench in the corner of the room by the front window and watch everyone wander around from niche to niche scrutinizing, touching, examining, shining, sampling, shaking and wearing. And even though Roland's lively talk and friendly advice were most welcome amid the uproar caused by his singular generosity, all the townspeople knew that the proprietor was never himself so content as when he was able to sit calmly by the window and watch the whirlwind of joy and amusement pass before his eyes.

It was never quite clear to anyone why Roland gave away his precious belongings like this. Just as it was never quite clear why he was so happy all the time. Almost every year someone would allude to the unusualness of Roland's behavior and say something like, "Awfully nice of you, Roland, but I hope your wife doesn't mind..." or "You certainly have a beautiful selection this year, Roland, but I'm surprised you haven't sold anything in Frankfurt..." or "Marvelous quality, my friend. However, I know how you could easily make ten times the cost..." or "Doesn't it get to you sometimes, Roland old man?" or "Are you sure you don't mind parting with this one too?" or more and more of the same. Usually Roland would just grin silently at these remarks. But though he certainly was an enigmatic character, the happy merchant was not in the least unnecessarily secretive, and more than once he explained the reasons for his generosity and his perpetual happiness to one of his many acquaintances. His conversation would usually go something like this:

"Well, the answer is rather simple really: it is necessary for me to repay the Giver of Gifts. And what more appropriate way to do this than by giving. He must feel as happy in His giving as I do in mine—even more so, really, because He is so much more generous. Who is the Giver of Gifts, you seem to ask with that puzzled look on your face? Well, I don't really know who He is. I've never actually met Him. Only I cannot help feeling overwhelmed by His—I am almost inclined to say—'outlandish' generosity. We receive a gift every moment. Every moment. You see it? Look at those little arms of sunlight playing on that purple cushion, with flecks of dust gently floating through them. Now, look at that gray cat scratching his forehead. Oh! Now look, see that adorable little girl standing in the corner of the room trying on that enormous pink hat with the green feathers? She thinks no one notices her. How sweet... Now! See that! A father and son are carrying that heavy wooden chest out the front door.

How patient they are with each other, how—Oh! Listen to the church bell in the next town! So rich and solemn. It must be a funeral. Ah, the fragrant sandalwood—can you smell it? I'm so glad I purchased that last week. And aren't these cakes delightful? Hilda baked them especially for today. And this chair is so relaxing. It is wonderful for the back. When I finish my tea, we must put it alongside the other ones. Such an unusual cloud formation now. You see the outline of gold and pink haze? How serious Arthur appears today. Look at him. I think he will notice the spade before too long. It is just right for him. Oh, now listen to that music box over there. Rather a peculiar melody..."

Roland's delight quickly became everyone's delight, so it was easy for anyone to become readily charmed by his descriptions of the generosity of the Giver of Gifts. Even so, no one else could fully grasp who or what it was. This probably did not matter all that much because, as far as the townspeople were concerned, the happy shopkeeper himself was the giver of gifts.

After twenty-seven years of harmonious married life, Roland's dear Hilda passed away. His three children soon moved off to other parts of the country and started families of their own. Roland maintained his shop for another six years after his wife's death and reliably continued his days of gift giving. The only difference seemed to be that he had to bake the cakes and pastries himself. Then in the summer of that sixth year, the day before his July gift day, Roland died, rather suddenly but, as far as anyone could tell, perfectly at peace. Mr. Ashbourne, the locksmith, found the merchant lying on the floor by his work table, the victim of heart failure. The entire town mourned the good man's passing, and after a solemn and appropriately religious burial, they unanimously declared the fifteenth of July a public holiday. Roland's three children sold all of their father's remaining antiques at reduced prices and divided up the profits evenly. Mr. Ashbourne took over Roland's storefront for his own business. He had a special brass plaque fastened over the threshold with the following phrase engraved upon it in large gothic letters: "In memory of Roland, The Giver of Gifts."

People who had known him remembered Roland for a long time. It was almost impossible for someone to pass by the locksmith's shop window without conjuring up a picture of that round, smiling face with the jeweler's lens in his eye. And then they would remember him in many other simple moments: Roland bustling about the shop, Roland holding up and describing an unusual object, Roland handing out cakes, Roland pointing at the clouds, Roland tinkering with a broken pocketwatch, Roland listening to the birds sing. It was almost as though there had been no real difference between the impressions of any given moment and Roland's indication of them or reaction to them. During his lifetime this phenomenon had not struck any of the townspeople as being anything unusual. They simply enjoyed whatever he said or did. Probably because he always felt so very, very happy.

www.ingramcontent.com/pod-product-compliance
Lightning Source LLC
Chambersburg PA
CBHW072221170626
46813CB00003B/1043